Mina's

Joint 2

The Perfect Illusion

D1713449

Dedication

This book is dedicated to the loves of my life: my son, Kyrese, my best friends, Mo and Locia, the wonderful group of ladies that encourage me, Brenda, Jenni and Gaylene, my crazy family and you, my beautiful, loving, supportive readers. Without each and every one of you, there would be no me.

I wanna send a major thank you to the Color Me Pynk team - LaMia and Devenchi. We got another hit, guys!!! Love you both to pieces!!!

And a special shout out to one of my long-time readers and now friend, Cherita Merricks. This is book for you.

Xoxo,

Keisha

Intuition:

The ability to understand something immediately, without the need for conscious reasoning.

What are you doing, my love?

#1

"I'm sorry, Mr. and Mrs. Gonzalez, but your test results came back negative." Dr. Warren said, sympathetically.

No, this can't be happening to me again, Mina choked back her tears. Unable to breathe, she stared at the calendar. It was June 4, 2015. The day would forever be etched in her memory bank. It was the day the devil came knocking on her door, wreaking havoc, once again. For the past two years, she and Victor had been doing IVF treatments in order to conceive another child. The first time, after months of sticking herself with needles, completing egg retrieval and an embryo transfer, her pregnancy test results came back negative.

The second time, the process was a success but after three months, she miscarried; and now on her third try, once again, none of the embryos implanted. Hot tears scorched the rim of Mina's hazel eyes. Her worse nightmare was becoming her reality. If she wasn't able to carry another child, she honestly didn't know what she was going to do. Her family was her world. Raising Lelah and José was her greatest joy and biggest accomplishment in life. She would give every worldly possession she owned to have another baby.

Her whole life, Mina envisioned herself having a big family; but the way things were shaping up, it didn't look like her dream would come true. *Maybe it's all the stress,* she told herself. The last two years of her life had been the worst. She'd gone through hell and back trying to get pregnant again, only to have her heart shattered into pieces each time. Then out of nowhere, one day she woke up to find her husband, Victor, gone.

She received a phone call from him saying he'd be gone for a while and to call her brother-in-law, Black, for help. When Mina called Black like instructed, he informed her that Victor was in hiding because the Feds were closing in on him. Mina knew the day would come when their family would be in danger again. She'd dreaded it for years but swept her fears under the rug. She refused to live in fear. She was going to enjoy every second with her man and their two beautiful kids. But the fact that Victor was the head of the biggest drug cartel in America, loomed over their heads. Danger was imminent. They wouldn't be safe forever.

Her husband's drug empire was now worth over 700 million dollars. There was no way on God's green earth that he wouldn't eventually be touched or locked up. So when he disappeared like a thief in the night for six months, Mina's entire world instantly began to spin out of control. She didn't know how to live without her husband. He was her entire world. If he wasn't around, she didn't exist.

The six months he was gone was a blur. Mina took care of home, the kids, her salons, slept and drank herself to death while Black ran the cartel. She tried to remain sane but the task was damn near impossible. When Victor went into hiding, Mina had just miscarried the baby a week before. She hadn't even wrapped her head around what happened when she was dumped with his fleeing on her lap. It was all too much to handle.

Mina felt like a shell of herself. She couldn't eat and sleep became her best friend. A bottle of wine each night helped to numb the pain. Not a day went by that she wasn't in tears. She needed her man back. She needed him there to hold her at night. She needed him to ease the ache in her chest and fill the void of the baby, which was no longer in her stomach.

Living life without Victor was like a death sentence. She didn't know when, or if, he was coming back. It was torture. After six long months, he returned to her. It was the happiest day of her life, outside of marrying him. Mina made him swear that he'd never pull such a stunt again.

"Wherever you go, I go," she stressed.

Now here they were, three months later, trying to pick up where they left off. Mina turned and looked at Victor. She felt like she was drowning on the inside. She needed him to save her. Tears slipped out of the corner of her eyes and down her cheeks.

Victor gazed back at her with a frustrated expression on his face. He hated to see his wife so broken up. She'd had her hopes up that things would work out in their favor. It was starting to look like having another child wasn't in the cards for them. Victor held her hand tightly and gave her a look that said everything would be ok. Although, he didn't really know if that was true.

He could buy Mina the world 10 times over, but giving her another baby was the one thing he couldn't give her. As a man, he'd failed. Victor was a man with pride. Knowing that he couldn't fulfill a need for his wife tore him up inside. He'd give anything to make Mina happy. When she hurt, he hurt.

She was his rib, his best friend and the love of his life. They'd been together 10 years. It had been the best 10 years of his life. Mina made every day worth living. He wished he could fix this for her but Victor was tapped out. He had enough on his plate. He couldn't deal with the added stress of their infertility problems. Something had to give - and fast.

"I'm sorry, Mina. I know how bad you wanted this time to be a success," Dr. Warren continued. "You still have options. You can try again, do a surrogacy or adopt."

"No." Mina wiped her face. "We're going to try again. I'm not giving up."

Victor whipped his head in her direction. They'd discussed that if the results came back negative, they were done. But no, here Mina was trying to flip the script.

"I don't know what she's talkin' about, Doc, but we're done. It's a wrap," he rebutted.

"What do you mean we're done?" Mina looked at him confused.

"We discussed this, Mina. I'm not doing this no more. We're done." He said sternly.

"But I really feel like if we give it one more shot we can do this. It's not like I can't get pregnant—"

"I said," Victor glared at her. "We're done."

Mina sat silent. Victor had put his foot down. When he got like this, she knew there was no reasoning with him. She wanted to scream. She couldn't believe he was doing this to her. After being gone for six months with no form of communication, giving her another go at IVF was the least he could do. She'd damn near lost her mind while he was away. She had to suffer through miscarrying alone. It was taking everything in her not to explode. Mina pressed her lips together and tapped her foot repeatedly. She was so mad she couldn't think straight.

"Thank you for everything, Doc." Victor stood and shook Dr. Warren's hand. "C'mon, baby."

Mina didn't want to go. She knew if she walked out of the door she'd never see Dr. Warren again and her dream of being a mother again would die. Swallowing her agony and anger, she rose to her feet.

"You'll be hearing from me soon." She assured Dr. Warren, picking up her gray Celine purse.

Victor looked at her like she was crazy. She was basically saying fuck you, I'ma do what the hell I wanna to do. With the keys to his Lexus GS F Sedan in hand, Victor exited the building. The morning sun blared so bright it almost blinded him. Victor shielded his eyes with his hand and made his way over to the car. Their security detail was waiting in the parking lot. Mina followed behind him with her Thierry Lasry snobby, cat-eye sunglasses on. The sound of her Alia heels echoed off the pavement as she walked.

She was in no rush to get to the car. Mina was taking her sweet, precious time. She didn't even want to be around her husband. He'd destroyed what little hope she had left by shutting down any future appointments with Dr. Warren. Victor unlocked the door for her. Although he was upset with Mina, he'd never not be the gentleman his father taught him to be. It was embedded in his DNA.

Mina rolled her eyes and got inside. Victor closed the door behind her and got in as well. Angry, he placed his head back on the headrest. He didn't want to start an argument but Mina's little stunt needed to be discussed.

Resting her elbow on the armrest, she gazed out the window and sighed. She felt trapped.

"What was that about?" Victor finally asked.

"Not now, Victor. I don't feel like arguing with you." Mina responded, depleted.

"Who's arguing? I'm just asking you a question." He shot with an attitude.

"Well, I don't feel like answering it," Mina snapped.

"Yo, you can quit actin' like a fuckin' brat. Answer the question."

"What was what about?" Mina jerked her arms up and down, irritated.

Victor was working on her last nerve.

"Yo, you gon' piss me off for real. Quit actin' dumb. You know damn well what I'm talkin' about. We agreed that if it didn't work out this time we were done; but back in there you flipped the script and went rogue on me. I thought we were supposed to be a team?"

"Team?" Mina drew her head back, appalled.

"Were we a team when you hopped yo' ass up and left me for six months?" She finally gave him eye contact.

"Here you go with that shit again." Victor shook his head, wishing he hadn't said a word.

"You damn right, here I go again. I have every right to be upset. You left me! I didn't know where you were, who you were with or if you were alive or dead. Then you come back and everything is supposed to be alright? Nigga, please, life don't work that way. I had just had a fuckin' miscarriage. I needed you!"

"You know why I had to go."

"Yeah, well it don't make it right," Mina shrugged, taking off her shades.

Victor licked his bottom lip and tried to keep his composure.

"Look, I understand that you're mad, but I don't want to do this anymore. I'm mentally drained. I'm done trying."

"Ok, well maybe I don't want to stop." Mina spat as tears formed in her eyes.

She wished he could see how desperately she wanted to give birth to another little him. Victor was the love of her life. Every time she gazed into his brown eyes she fell in love all over again. He was the most stunning creature she'd ever seen. After 10 years together, he still made her feel like a little schoolgirl. She loved everything about him. There wasn't a flaw on him.

He was perfect in her eyes. Victor was her man crush every day. She thanked God every time she got to wake up to his handsome face. He was 6 feet of black and Latino wonder. He rocked his hair low with a part like Nas. His thick, bushy brows perfectly framed his diamond-shaped, brown eyes. He had a broad nose, sexy, full lips and a full, smooth beard that made her wet between the thighs. He rocked two small diamond earrings in each of his ears.

Victor was built like an African god. His daily visits to the gym had done his body good. He was a muscular 210 pounds. The man had an 8-pack for God's sake and Ken doll slits on his waist. A tattoo of a lion roaring with Lelah and José's name was etched into his right arm. On his back was her name. Mina couldn't get enough of him. Her husband was the shit. He gave her butterflies. No other man could make her feel the way he did. Victor was well aware of his sex appeal. He often used it to get what he wanted. Whenever Mina got out of hand, all he had to do was look at her and her juices would start flowing.

His dick game was mesmerizing. She stayed wanting the pipe. She had to have him morning, noon and night. He was the flavor she preferred. He stimulated her mind and kept her on her grind. His love took her higher than the sky. When he came around, she still got weak in the knees. Whenever she looked at their son's face, she saw a little version of him staring back at her. She'd wanted badly to experience that again.

"Victor, you know I always wanted to have another baby."

"I get that but, Mina, you're 36 years old—"

"And?" She looked him up and down.

"I'm 38. Nigga, we gettin' old. I ain't trying to be in my 50's with a teenager. The shit already hard as it is now," he stressed.

"What you mean it's already hard? You don't do shit wit' the kids, for real. I'm the one always with them. You too busy always workin'," she spat.

"That's a fucked-up-ass thing to say. I'm always there for my kids. If I don't work, yo' ass don't eat. And we both know how much yo' ass love to eat."

"Really?" Mina wanted to slap fire out of his mouth.

"You went there first. Don't ever question my fuckin' parenting skills. You the one walk around here acting like you're they father and mother. You act like you're the man of the house."

"Fuck all of that. Take back the fat joke," she commanded.

"What you mad for? You ain't even fat no more," Victor laughed.

"So! Take it the fuck back."

Despite the fact that she was skinny now, Mina would always feel like the fat, chubby girl she once was.

"I'm sorry." He kissed the back of her hand.

Mina rolled her eyes at him, still pissed.

"For real tho'. You know how bad it fucks me up every time we fail at this shit? I can't see you hurt no more. It's too much."

"Baby, I understand." She turned around in her seat and faced him. "It hurts. It hurts like a muthafucka, but I'd go through it time and time again to have another baby with you," she cried.

"You act like we ain't got kids," he argued. "Lelah is about to start college next year. José is 10 going on 30. We good. It's time we focus on us. I don't wanna start all over again. I got enough shit going on in my life right now. The situation I'm dealing with ain't over wit' yet." Victor referred to the federal investigation. "Plus, my new club just opened up. I gotta make sure that's straight."

"I'm so sick of your problems being my problem. I've dedicated the last 10 years of my life to you. When is it going to be about me and what I want for once? Anything you've ever asked of me, I've done. I have lived my life underneath a microscope. I can't go here. I can't go there. I can't do this. I can't do that. My house is like freaking Fort Knox. Every day I'm surrounded by security guards. I gotta constantly look over my shoulder to make sure that somebody that hates you don't try to kill me—"

"Don't throw that shit up in my face. You knew what the fuck you was gettin' into when you married me. Now you wanna question our life? Now you wanna act like what I do is such a fuckin' problem to you? I don't see you complaining when you fuckin' up Bergdorf or Saks Fifth Avenue. You sure don't complain when we vacation overseas every summer. It's all good then," he mocked.

"And if what I do is so fuckin' dangerous, then why would you want to add another kid to the situation? That don't even make no sense."

"Because this ain't about you! It's about me!" Mina yelled.

She didn't know how to tell her husband that ever since he went away and returned, she felt like a piece of him was missing. He'd come back still in his physical form, but something wasn't quite the same. Mina couldn't put her finger on what the change was. All she knew for sure was that something in her spirit didn't feel right.

Her need to have another child increased every time she felt another piece of him slip away. Maybe if they had another baby they'd grow close again. She couldn't tell him she was desperate to save their marriage and that she thought having a baby would solve their problems.

"I don't know what to tell you then." Victor started up the car.

He was over the conversation and done with IVF.

"Today was my last day coming here."

"Whatever, Victor." Mina placed her shades back on. "I'ma have me another baby."

"Something don't feel right because it ain't right. Especially coming up after midnight."

-Beyoncé, "Hold Up"

#2

Walking from room to room, Mina turned off each light. The house was silent. The only sound she could hear was the sound of her feet slapping against the LuxTouch tiled floors. It was the most expensive tile in the world. Each tile was inlaid with 95 brilliant cut diamonds in a sumptuous flower petal pattern surrounding a rich, black, agate circle. Each corner was inlaid with Abalone Shell and mother-of-pearl, creating a stunning overall effect. Every 10 square feet of LuxTouch tile cost $1 million dollars.

Victor's drug money afforded them the ability to live in the lap of luxury. They had the poshest home in St. Louis. Their family lived on a 20-acre compound that was worth 63 million dollars. The mansion had 7 bedrooms, 18 bathrooms, an in-home salon, 3 elevators, library, media screening and projector room, bowling alley, outdoor pool, basketball court and a 17-car garage. But having the dopest house didn't stop the fact that it was almost 2:00am and Victor still wasn't home.

The writing was on the wall but Mina couldn't see the words. Her vision was blurred. She didn't want to believe that her marriage was in jeopardy. Mina and Victor had barely spoken since the doctor's appointment earlier that day. She didn't mind it much. She needed time to gather her thoughts. Mina loved the quiet of night. It was the only time she had a moment to herself.

The kids were asleep. The house staff had gone home, but security still lingered inside and outside their home. Mina hated that she never had her house to herself but it was a part of the game. Victor wasn't going to risk her being kidnapped again. Being a drug kingpin had already cost him his daughter, Lelah's mother. He wasn't going to lose Mina too. He'd lose his shit if anything ever happened to her and the kids.

Emotionally drained, Mina headed to her bedroom. Being alone had become the norm for her. Even with Victor being back, he was still gone. He was hardly ever home. When he was, there was distance between them. The feeling was unexplainable.

He still doted on her and showered her with love and affection, but Mina could feel it in the air, something had changed. It was as if he saw past her now. She used to look in his eyes and see her reflection but now nothing was there. Mina stood in the doorway of her bedroom and looked around.

The whole room had a neutral color palette. The ceilings were painted white and the walls a shade of taupe. In the center of the room was their custom-designed, king-sized bed. The square-shaped, tufted headboard was made out of gray suede. On each side of the bed was a set of crème nightstands. A taupe, Victorian-inspired chaise sat in front of the bed. Off to the right was a nice, little, cozy corner where she could sit and read her favorite Keisha Ervin novels. She decorated the space with an oversized chair, ottoman and plant. An antique Tiffany chandelier hung from the ceiling. Two Jackson Pollack paintings decorated the walls.

Bay windows gave them the perfect view of their backyard and pool. Everything was pristine and luxurious, just how Mina liked it. Dressed in a crème, silk negligee, she stood in front of the full-length mirror and examined herself. Mina didn't even recognize herself anymore. All of her womanly curves were gone. She was no longer the size 16, curvaceous diva she once was. Cutting out meat, taking daily shots, being stressed out and lovesick had changed her appearance.

She was now a size 10. Despite her drastic weight loss, Mina was still that bitch. Long, thick, black hair draped past her shoulders and down to her butt. She was 5'8 with butterscotch skin, hazel eyes and pink, luscious lips. People often mistook her for her superfamous sister, Meesa. Mina's 34C breasts sat up firmly. For the first time in her life, she had a flat stomach and a firm, round ass.

Mina didn't know who she was anymore. She missed who she used to be. She missed having a baby in her stomach. Mina ran her hand across her lower abdomen and imagined being pregnant. Tears filled her eyes. Life wasn't fair. It had chewed her up and spit her out into a million pieces. She was desperately screaming out for help but no one could hear her. She was alone.

Tired of looking at the imposter in the mirror, she got into bed. Mina picked up her phone to see if Victor had called. He hadn't. It was 1:57am on a Friday morning and he was still at the club. Victor had formed a club empire. He had several extremely successful clubs all over the world. Victor had clubs in St. Louis, L.A., Miami, New York, Paris and Dubai. He'd cornered the market and made millions. He could easily retire and live off the club money for the rest of his life, but the street life wouldn't let him go.

Mina didn't know how much longer she'd be willing to live the lifestyle. Victor had promised that by the time he was 35 he'd retire, but here they were, still knee-deep in the drug game. Mina didn't know how many more sleepless, fearful nights she could take. She wanted peace and a peace of mind. She wanted her husband to herself. Mina was tired of sharing him with the world. He was hers. The only problem was that Victor liked living life in the fast lane. He got an adrenaline rush out of being the El Chapo of the United States.

He didn't see how his career choice was affecting his wife. She was sick of him always being away. Mina was a homebody. Her days of kicking it at the club until the wee hours of the morning were over. She liked spending her nights at home with her children. The only thing missing was Victor. But this was the life she'd signed up for. When she pledged her love for him before God, she swore to support his dreams, even though she didn't necessarily agree with some of his choices. She wished he would give her the same courtesy and support her quest of bringing another life into the world.

Mina turned off the bedside lamp and lay on her side. Through the darkness, she stared at a wedding photo of them. *We were so happy then,* she thought as she heard Victor come up the steps. Mina quickly closed her eyes and pretended to be sleep. Not wanting to disturb his wife, Victor crept into their bedroom quietly.

He didn't even bother to turn the lights on. He knew Mina worked hard and needed her rest. Victor sat on his side of the bed and looked over his shoulder at her. Mina's back faced him. He loved to watch her sleep. She always looked so peaceful and serene. He was happy she was knocked out. He didn't feel like hearing her mouth about him coming in late. He'd argued with her enough that day.

Little did Victor know, but Mina was wide awake. She was pissed. She didn't understand why he was coming in the house at two o'clock in the morning. Wasn't nothing open at the time of morning but legs. He didn't need to be at the club. His ass needed to be home! He had managers to handle the clubs' everyday business. It made no sense for him to be gone every night. He should've been home with her and their kids.

Victor acted like she hadn't gotten the worse news of her life earlier that day. Did he not care that she was hurting or was he trying to numb his own pain by staying away? Mina listened closely as he took his clothes off. She didn't know if she was losing her shit, but she swore she smelled the scent of another woman's perfume in the air. Her heart began to race a mile a minute. Her head was racing. She wanted to roll over and confront him, but what if he'd gotten the scent on him when he hugged someone?

Mina didn't want to come off looking like a crazy woman. This was her husband she was questioning. Victor had never given her a reason to doubt his fidelity. That didn't stop the nagging feeling in the center of her chest. The fear inside of Mina grew as she heard him get up, go in the bathroom and turn on the shower.

Normally, she wouldn't have tripped, but Victor had taken a shower before he left. *What are you doing, my love,* she thought, sitting up alarmed. *Is this nigga cheating on me? Nah, he can't be,* she told herself as her heart thumped loudly. *Mina, you're trippin'. Victor ain't cheating on you.* Needing confirmation, she pulled the covers off her body, reached over and grabbed his shirt. The smell of his Tom Ford Noir cologne engulfed her nose. Mina could no longer trace the scent of the perfume.

Mina didn't know what to do. She hadn't been in this position since she left her ex-fiancé, Andrew. Should she act off emotion or fall back and gather more information? Mina closed her eyes and thought for a second. *C'mon, girl, pull it together. You've had a rough day. Victor loves you. Nothing is going on.* Opening her eyes, she placed his shirt back on the bed and went inside the bathroom.

She watched as Victor stood underneath the shower head with his arms pressed against the wall. His head was down. Streams of water ran over his body. He seemed overwhelmed, like he had the weight of the world on his shoulders. Mina began to feel horrible. Here she was thinking he was cheating when it was obvious that the day's events had affected him too. As his wife, she should've realized that her inability to get pregnant wasn't just a burden on her.

It affected him too. Mina often forgot that Victor lived a very complicated life. Every day he wore a mask. To the world, he was a club mogul, husband and father; but to the underworld, he was Victor Gonzalez, a savage drug dealer and killer. Victor had to be everything to everyone. He needed her support just as much as she needed his.

Mina wanted to be selfish and only worry about her needs but being selfish wasn't in her DNA.

She was devoted to her husband and their marriage… Despite them being at a crossroads. They'd figure their way out of the madness. They'd done it before. One at a time, she pushed the spaghetti straps of her negligee past her shoulders and allowed it to fall to the floor. She needed Victor in the worst way. Mina opened the shower door and stepped into the hot steam.

Victor was so deep in thought, he didn't even hear her come in. Mina stood behind her husband and examined his muscular back. Her name was tattooed across his shoulder blades in big, bold letters. Beads of water trickled down his back. Mina inched closer and pressed the side of her face against his spine. Her arms were wrapped around his waist. Victor relished the feel of her hand on his skin.

He'd had a long, exhausting day. If Mina knew half the shit he was dealing with, she'd understand why he was so different. He knew she knew he'd changed, but Victor wasn't ready to reveal what plagued him. What he was dealing with was far too complicated to just explain. He needed time. Until he was ready to talk verbally, he'd show her his emotions sexually.

Victor turned and faced her. Mina's breasts were now pressed up against his chest. She looked so sexy standing there. Finally, her guard was down and he could have his way with her. The last thing Victor wanted to do was argue and fight. He wanted to make love to her. Mina was his kryptonite. He could never get his full of her. Victor turned her around and made her switch positions with him.

The hot and steamy water now cascaded down her face. Her hair clung to the back of her neck. Mina looked like a goddess. She stood before him massaging his hard dick. Her hands glided up and down his long pole with velvet ease. The hardness of his cock almost made Mina cum. Gazing into his eyes, she got down on her knees and took him into her wanting mouth.

Victor watched as his dick slid in and out of her mouth. Mina sucked his dick like a pro. She knew exactly how to make him go insane. Victor's dick was so hard he thought it was going to break. The warmth of her mouth on his cock as she tortured him was mind-blowing. Victor didn't want her to stop. Being with her this way took away all of his stress. If they got down like this more often, then maybe they wouldn't be at each other's throats so much.

Mina loved the taste of her husband's dick in her mouth. It fit perfectly. Wet as hell, she bobbed her head back and forth while stroking his shaft with her hands. Victor's eyes rolled to the back of his head. Swiftly, he scooped her up in his big, strong arms and placed her legs on his shoulders. He had to taste her. Mina's sweet nectar lathered his tongue like honey.

She was decadent. Victor let his tongue travel up and down her wet slit. Mina tilted her head back and moaned. This was what she needed. No matter what the problem was, Victor always knew how to make her feel better.

"Ooooooh, baby," she gasped as he circled his tongue around her clit. "Yeah, just like that."

Victor wanted to make sure she was nice and wet before he took her from behind. While sucking on her clit, he fingered her pussy. Mina was in heaven. This was the best she'd felt in a long while. Victor's tongue was working magic on her pussy. Mina looked on in agony as his mouth engulfed her clit. Victor was eating her so well, she unintentionally began to ride his face.

"Fuck, baby!" She shuddered, rocking her hips back and forth.

"You like that?" He smacked her ass.

"Yessssss," Mina whined. "Victor, it feels so good."

"You want this dick, don't you?"

"Yesssssss." Mina licked her lips.

Victor placed her down and made her face the shower door. Mina's breasts were pressed up against the glass. Victor slid his dick inside her pussy while toying with her clit. The sound of his pelvis slapping against her ass echoed in the air.

"Fuck," he groaned.

Mina's pussy was the best. The deeper he went, the harder his dick became.

"Ooooooooh! Oh God!"

"Ahhhhhh," Victor groaned. "Se siente bien?"

"Yes! Baby, it feels so good!"

"Aww shit." Victor watched her ass bounce.

"Ooh, Victor, you got me so wet." Mina moaned as he rocked inside her. "Victor, baby, please, I'ma cum."

"Usted gon semen para papá"

"Mmmm hmmm! I'ma cum for you, daddy!" Mina loved when Victor spoke in Spanish to her.

"Turn around," he demanded.

Mina did as she was told.

"Wrap your legs around me." Victor picked her up.

Mina's back was pressed against the shower door.

"Pull me in… pull me in… pull me in," she whimpered.

"You gon' cum long and hard on this dick?"

"Mmmm hmmmmm!" Mina's legs began to quiver. "Yessssssssssssssssssssssss!"

"You love this dick, don't you?" He pulled her into him with brute force.

"I love this dick! Oooh, I love it so much."

Mina's titties bounced up and down. She could barely keep up with Victor. He was fucking her so good.

"You gon' love me forever?" He questioned, hitting her with the death stroke.

"Nigga, I'ma love you till the day I die." Mina's eyes fluttered as she came all over his dick.

"I smell your secret."

-Beyoncé, "Hold Up"

#3

Mornings at the Gonzalez estate was always a mad house. There was always something going on or someone around doing something. On an everyday basis, there was a maid, butler, driver, gardener and personal trainer at their home. Mina ran around like a chicken with its head cut off. She didn't believe in nannies or chefs so she did everything herself. She made it her business to cook her family breakfast and dinner no matter how busy she was. She ran herself dizzy but her family was her number one priority.

Breakfast was normally the only time of the day she got to spend any time with Victor. Most of the time, they were like two ships passing in the night. When he came home, she was asleep; and when she got home from work, he was gone to the club or out handling business. If she didn't have a constant reminder of her 10 carat wedding ring on her hand, Mina would've swore she was a single mother.

The kids barely ever got to spend any one-on-one time with their father anymore. Lelah was 17 and practically out the door so she didn't care. She spent the majority of her time plastered to her phone, Snapchatting and kicking it with her friends. Lelah was a good girl though. Victor and Mina didn't have any problems out of her. She was your typical teenage girl. She was obsessed with her looks, boys and clothes.

Her beauty was timeless. She'd grown into quite the young lady. Most people mistook her for Evelyn Lozada's daughter, Shanice. Lelah's caramel skin complimented her perfectly-arched brows, slanted, brown eyes and silky, black hair. Lelah had several piercings in her ears that her father couldn't stand. It took a lot of convincing on Mina's part to persuade Victor to allow her to get them. Her bright, Colgate smile lit up an entire room. She was tall, reaching 5'10 in height.

To be only 17, Lelah had a banging body. She was very fit, as she ran track at Waverly High. The more her body developed, the more Victor lost his mind. He hated to see his baby girl grow up. He wanted her to stay little forever. She could've been a model but her dream was to become a pediatrician.

Whenever Lelah needed help or advice, she went straight to Mina. Mina wasn't her biological mother but she'd helped raise her since she was seven years old. She was the only mother figure Lelah knew, besides her grandmother, Faith.

She even called her mom. Mina was right there by her side when she got her first crush, period, bought her first bra and experienced her first heartbreak. Lelah couldn't ask for a better mother. Mina never tried to push herself on Lelah. She let their relationship progress naturally. Mina was always there waiting in the wings. She didn't give birth to Lelah, but in her eyes, they were blood.

She didn't consider Lelah her stepdaughter; she was her child. She was there whenever she got sick. When she broke her arm jumping off a swing playing, Mina was the one who sat at the emergency room with her for five hours. Mina attended every dance recital and parent-teacher conference. She taught Lelah how to do her hair and makeup and conduct herself like a lady.

Mina loved Lelah with every fiber of her being. When it was time for her to go away to school, she didn't know how she was going to cope. Lelah was just playing with Barbie dolls; now she was going into her senior year. Thankfully, Mina still had her little one. Although there was nothing little about José. He was big in every sense of the word. He had a big personality, a big mouth and a big appetite just like his mother. José was the cutest, chubbiest, 10-year-old boy on the planet.

He had a thick, curly fro and the smoothest butterscotch skin. He was the perfect mixture of his father and mother. José possessed brown, doe-shaped eyes. He was a short little man reaching only 4 feet 8 in height. He still had a little baby fat on him. Mina loved the extra meat on his bones. She knew when he got older the weight would fall off. José was always giving unsolicited advice and speaking out of term, but his brash personality is what made him unique. He was fearless, just like his father.

Mina hovered over the kitchen stove trying to make pancakes, eggs and sausage but flashbacks of the night before danced in her head. With all of the IVF treatments, it had been a minute since she and Victor had an all-out freak session. Back in the day they weren't able to keep their hands off one another. They always got it poppin'. Over the years, life got in the way of intimacy. Mina longed for the days where they would lay up in bed and fuck all day. In order to do that, her husband would have to be around more.

For the longest, she tried to act like everything was ok but the cracks in their relationship were starting to show.

She couldn't drink, smoke, shop or sleep the problem away. The fact that her marriage was on shaky ground rocked her to the core. She didn't know when things went left. She couldn't dodge it anymore. Maybe this was their season to be tested.

"And if I hit the switch, I can make that ass drop." José rapped along to Ice Cube's Today Was A Good Day.

"You better watch your mouth, li'l boy." Mina looked over her shoulder at him.

"I'm practicing, Ma. I gotta be on point for the summer camp talent show. I can't let Aaron beat me again this year."

"I don't give a damn if you were performing in front of the Pope. Don't let me catch you cussin' again."

"Why not? Granny let me cuss at her house all the time," José argued.

"I ain't your granny, and besides, your granny is crazy. Now sit yo' narrow ass down so you can eat this food I'm cooking. We gotta be outta here in a minute."

"Ma, you actin' real light skin right now." José shook his head.

"Say something else," Mina warned. "And I'ma whoop yo' butt."

"Ma, you know you can't whoop me. The last time you tried, you started cryin' and put yourself on punishment."

Mina wanted to put him in his place but José was right. She hated to see her baby boy in any kind of pain, especially if the pain was inflicted by her. Now Victor, on the other hand, didn't have any problem disciplining. José feared his father and didn't try him like he did Mina.

"Shut up for I slap you." She rolled her eyes and tried her best not to laugh.

"Mmm… baby, you got it smelling good up in here." Victor strolled over and kissed her on the cheek. "I'm hungry than a muthafucka." He rubbed his stomach.

Mina eyed her husband. He was still dressed in his robe. A sliver of his tattooed chest peeked through the opening of his robe. Mina's panties instantly got wet. *This fine muthafucka,* she thought. Victor looked a lot like the guy that played Benny on Tyler Perry's The Haves and The Have Nots.

"Babe, you need any help?" He asked.

"No. I got it."

Victor shook his head. Whenever he offered Mina assistance she always refused. Victor wished she'd let him lead his household like a man was supposed to do.

"What up, Pop?" José dapped his dad up.

"Don't what up Pop me. Give me a hug, big head." Victor wrapped his son up in his arms.

José hugged his dad back, lovingly. He idolized his father.

"Let me look at you." Victor stood back and held him by the sides of his face. "You need a haircut, boy."

"Nah, I'm doing my Kevin Durant thing right now."

"You can do your Kevin Durant thing when you get you some Kevin Durant money. I'ma have the barber come by later today to hook you up."

"Eh, pero yo no quiero que mi corte de pelo," José poutcd.

"I don't care what you want. No son of mine is going to be walkin' around here with his hair looking like that," Victor shot.

"You and Mom gon' get me one day." José sat back down. "Ay yo ma, what's up wit' the pancakes? I'm starving here." He did his best impersonation of an Italian accent.

"I'm almost done," Mina lied.

She was only on her second pancake and the sausage had just started frying. She was running hella late. She and José would have to be out the house in 30 minutes in order for him to make it to summer camp and her to work on time. Lelah switched into the kitchen with her face buried inside her iPhone. She looked into her camera phone and made a duck face to take a selfie.

"I mean, if I get any prettier, I'ma get arrested," she gushed. "Daddy, thank you for my good looks."

"Oh, Lord, here she go," Victor chuckled, drinking a glass of orange juice.

"Pops." She continued to pose for a picture.

"Yes, Lelah?"

"Let me hold 300 dollars."

"What am I? A walking ATM? Don't you have a job?"

"Yeah, but your money is my spending money and the money I make, I save." She flipped her long hair to the side.

"Get your daughter." Victor said to Mina.

"You know you gon' give it to her." Mina quickly beat four eggs in a bowl.

"You better be glad you're my baby girl." Victor reached inside the pocket of his robe and peeled off $300.

Victor kept money on him at all times.

"Thank you, Daddy." Lelah kissed her father on the cheek and sat beside her brother.

"Ay yo, Pop." José leaned over. "Let me hold a stack. I got this li'l chick at camp I'm tryin' to scoop up."

"Who is this guy?" Victor laughed as his phone vibrated.

"He's a li'l badass. That's what he is." Lelah mushed her little brother in the head.

"Don't make me DDT you, girl." José pushed her back.

"Mom, you better get him before I hurt him." Lelah balled up her fist. "That's why you still pee in the bed."

"No, I don't! Shut up, li'l dusty foot. You can't talk about nobody. You still stuff yo' bra."

"Lies you tell. My boobs are perfect." Lelah pushed her breasts up.

"What boobs? Your chest is as flat as one of Rihanna's high notes," José joked.

"Don't talk about RiRi. Rihanna is my idol."

"Sure she is, THOT'Lelah," José cracked up laughing.

"Ma, please get your badass son. He's gettin' on my nerves."

"You started it!" José quipped.

"Will you two stop?" Mina turned around, exasperated. "José, what did I tell you about your mouth?"

"She started it."

Mina stared at Victor and wondered why he wasn't jumping in. He saw her trying to fix breakfast. The least he could do was keep the kids in line. Instead, he was all in his phone, texting someone. Mina was dying to know who was so goddamn important. It was 8:00 in the morning. Who was he talking to? It was as if he'd blocked the whole world out. He hadn't looked up from his phone once. He didn't even peep her glaring at him.

The longer he ignored the kids, the madder she became. Here she was slaving over a hot stove, fuckin' up her edges, and he sat his ass on the phone like he didn't have a care in the world. Victor needed to be more present. She was fed up with doing all the heavy lifting. He had a six-month vacation. It was time he focused on her and the kids. Needing to know what was going on, Mina placed the spatula down, walked over and wrapped her arm around his shoulder.

"Who textin' us?" She asked.

"What you talkin' about?" Victor placed his phone on the table face down.

His gesture didn't go unnoticed by Mina. *What the fuck is he hiding,* she wondered. She could smell his secrets and lies. It was killing her that she was in the dark.

"You cheating on me?" She blurted, out of nowhere.

The room instantly fell silent. The kids stopped arguing and looked at her. Victor furrowed his brows.

"Yo, you trippin'." He shook his head, shocked by her question.

Mina quickly realized she'd fucked up. She felt the sting of her words as they hung in the balance. She had no business asking him something like that in front of their kids. They'd been through enough over the last year. When their dad went away it hurt them too. They didn't know if they were ever going to see him again. Mina was spiraling out of control. She wasn't in her right mind. She didn't know if it was the hormones she'd been taking or her sneaking suspicions, but she was emotionally all over the place.

Tears rose in her eyes. Just as she was about to breakdown and cry, the smoke detector went off. She'd completely forgotten about the pancakes. She and Victor leaped to attention and ran over to the stove. The pancakes were burnt to a crisp. Mina turned the eye off.

"Move out the way, babe, I got it." Victor tried to take over.

"I got it!" Mina pushed him out the way.

Not paying attention, she tried to grab the handle but it was scolding hot.

"Oww, fuck!" She jerked her hand back, wagging it in the air.

"See, I told you! You fuckin' hardheaded." Victor stepped in with a pot holder and placed the pan in the sink.

Angry with herself, Mina rushed out of the kitchen and into the bathroom. Running her hand underneath some cold water, she looked at herself in the mirror. She was losing it. Mina had to get it together before she did something she'd regret. If Victor wasn't cheating on her, then he for sure was going to start if she kept it up.

But what was she to do when his personality wasn't clear? He was at arm's reach but she couldn't get a hold of him. She couldn't help but make things up in her mind. He was hiding something from her. She knew it. It made no sense that she still felt lonely even when he was around. Mina was an emotional wreck. Her hormones were in overdrive. She needed time to grieve the baby she lost and the fact that the IVF treatment was a complete failure but life wouldn't allow it. She was constantly being pulled in every direction. *God, help me.*

Victor walked into the bathroom and closed the door behind him. Stress was written all over Mina's face. He felt responsible. It was his fault she was crumbling but Victor loved her from her hair follicles all the way down to her toe nails.

"You a'ight?" He asked, looking at her through the bathroom mirror.

"No." Mina shook her head, somberly.

"You need a spa day or something, 'cause what you just did back there was crazy. Why would you ask me some shit like that?"

"I don't know," she sniffed. "I just feel like something is going on between us. Are we ok? Do I need to be worried?"

Victor made her turn around and face him.

"Baby, I love you. You know that."

"I get that but what you fail to realize is that I need you right now. I'm dying on the inside and I need you to catch me and lift me up," she cried. "It's like you're here but you're not here. I need for you to take the time to think about my feelings a little more."

"Mina, baby, I understand that you feeling some type of way right now." Victor wiped her tears. "But you need to understand that I'm going through some shit too. Shit you could never understand—"

"I can't understand if you don't talk me," she cut him off. "You used to tell me everything. We never kept secrets from one another. I'm trying to figure out what happened to my best friend 'cause it seems like somebody has taken my place."

"Cut it out. Ain't nobody takin' yo' place."

"That's what your mouth say but your actions are saying different. I try to do everything I can for you, Victor, and it all goes unnoticed. I put my body through hell for the last two years just to give you another baby but you don't care. You want me to be this understanding, supportive wife but you can't even acknowledge the fact that you left me for six months right after I had a fuckin' miscarriage," Mina's bottom lip quivered.

"Do you get that I didn't talk to or see you for six months? That shit ain't normal. But I had to accept it 'cause I'm married to a fuckin' drug dealer."

"Yo, chill." Victor screwed up his face.

He didn't want to take the risk that the kids might hear their conversation. As far as they knew, their father was strictly just a club owner.

"No, I won't chill," Mina spat. "Ever since you came back you've been mean, you've been cold and you've been distant. I don't know who you are anymore."

Victor licked his lips and looked off to the side. He heard his wife's cries loud and clear but the damage had already been done. There was no stopping what was transpiring between them. All he could do was try his best to slow down the train wreck before they flew off the rails.

"I know I be puttin' you through a lot. I don't be tryin' to, but I'm always thinkin' about business and what move I need to make next. I don't be trying to put my business over my personal life. But it's not just you and the kids that I support. Since my father died, I've had to be the man of my family. All I know how to do is hustle and focus on the paper. I try to be a fuckin' family man, but it's hard to concentrate when you gotta wonder if you gon' make it home alive every day," Victor stressed.

"I know I can be an asshole sometimes. But I don't want you to think that I'm just out here being selfish and not giving a fuck. I'm tryin' to survive and make sure we straight so I can come home to you every night. You and the kids are my life. I love you more than I could love anything in this world." Victor assured, running his fingers through her hair.

Being all in his feelings wasn't something he was used to, or particularly good at, but it truly broke his heart to see the agony he was taking Mina through. She deserved better.

"I love you too." Mina kissed him lovingly on the lips.

Seeing Victor get emotional tugged on her heart strings. It was rare that he let his emotions show.

"I'm sorry." She spoke just above a whisper. "I hear everything you're sayin. I just had to get that off my chest.

"It's cool. You've been dealing with a lot. I know you think you tough and shit 'cause you grew up on the Northside but, baby, you ain't invincible. You ain't superwoman. It's ok to be vulnerable. I got you." Victor gave her a soft kiss on the lips.

In that moment, Mina remembered that Victor really did love her. Their love was set in stone. He'd proven himself loyal throughout the years. She had no reason to question his commitment to her. They were just going through a little rough patch. Maybe it was a good thing she wasn't pregnant. Mina could wean herself off the hormones and focus on fixing their marriage.

"I'm serious though. You need to relax. I'ma have Julisa set up a spa day for you and your homegirls."

Julisa was Victor's longtime employee. She'd been loyal to Victor and their family. Because of her loyalty, she was promoted from being their maid to Victor's assistant. Mina was so proud of Julisa. She deserved the promotion.

"You're my baby." He rubbed her booty.

"Stop rubbing on my booty. You gon' make me horny," she laughed.

"You know you want this dick," Victor bit her neck. "You wanna go upstairs and have a repeat of last night?"

"I want to so bad, but I gotta drop the boy off and get to the shop." Mina poked out her bottom lip.

"You sure?" He pressed his hard dick up against her thigh.

Mina's knees buckled. She hated the effect Victor had on her. But she had to remain strong. She had to get to work.

"Later, baby." She pushed him back so she wouldn't change her mind.

"Can't you see there's no other man above you?"

-Beyoncé, "Hold Up"

#4

Mina pulled up in front of her main salon and parked her silver Bentley Continental GT Speed. Every time she visited one of her salons, she felt like a boss bitch. Mina had accomplished a lot. She'd turned her salon into a 7-million-dollar empire. She went from having one salon in the Delmar Loop to 10, walk-in, weave spots around St. Louis. She was working on her first children's beauty and barber shop. Business was booming. She'd even began to sell her own brand of hair. Luscious Hair couldn't stay on the shelves.

To go from being a poor little black girl from the hood to a mogul was a dream come true. Sometimes she couldn't believe her own luck. All the hard work and dues she paid over the years had paid off. She'd done it all by herself. She could've easily lived off Victor's money and enjoyed being a kept woman. Mina wanted to show not only herself, but her kids, to never rest on their laurels but to create a path of their own. She also wanted to show her husband that she didn't need his paper. She had her own.

Mina's mother raised her to be self-sufficient. If anything ever happened between her and Victor, she could easily chuck his ass up the deuce and bounce. She'd been stuck in a situation in the past with her ex where she had to depend on him to survive. Mina swore to never place herself in that position again. No man would have that much control over her life.

When she was with Andrew, he told her how to walk, talk, dress, and behave. She couldn't have a thought or an opinion of her own. If she did speak up for herself, she'd get slapped or punched. Each hit was a reminder that she was at his will. Whatever Andrew said or did couldn't be challenged because he supplied her with the funds to start Mina's Joint Salon and Spa. After a horrific break up that landed her in the hospital, Mina was able to take full ownership of her salon.

Mina chirped the alarm on her car and sauntered inside the shop. It was Friday so the place was packed. The smell of hair being pressed straight filled the air. This was home. Being at the salon was her calming place. Mina's Joint was like the black Cheers. Everybody knew your name. There was always something chaotic going on.

Somebody's business was always getting told and her lead stylist, Delicious, was probably the one spilling the tea.

What Mina loved the most was the new décor. She'd had the whole place remodeled. The ceilings were made of mirrored tile. A $200,000 crystal chandelier hung from the center, giving the salon an opulent appeal. The walls were gold and white. Each station had white, oval-shaped, ceiling to floor mirrors. All of the salon chairs were white, sleek and chic. The black, slick floor set the entire space off. The shop was exquisite and worth every dime she'd spent.

"Mina!" The staff and clients yelled.

"Well looky-looky-looky. Here come Cookie." Delicious popped his lips. "Yo' ass is late! Had me coming up in here at the crack of dawn and yo' ass ain't even show up for your appointment. You know damn well a bitch need her beauty rest."

"Good morning to you too, Delicious." Mina ignored his sarcasm.

She was used to Delicious being overdramatic. Everything about him was over-the-top. Delicious was tall, slim, and chocolate, with a sickening blonde buzz cut and grey contacts. He had a surgically-enhanced ass that was so fat even Serena Williams would be jealous. That day, he wore a gold chain with Delicious written across the name plate, a black, leather crop top, leather, pleated skirt, knee-high socks and Tims.

"Uh ah, Miss Mina, I ain't letting you get off that easy." He switched over and stood by her. "I was trying to get my back cracked this morning before Waymon went out of town."

"Didn't you just find out that he was married to some Puerto Rican broad?" Mina looked over the mail.

"Yeah, adulterer." Jodie, the receptionist and devote Christian, hissed.

"Didn't nobody ask you nothing, Church of Latter Day Saints. Don't judge me. You don't know my life. If you got a taste of his dick you would want to keep it in your mouth too," Delicious snapped his finger.

"That's enough, Delicious!" Mina gasped. "We got kids in here." She looked over at the 16-year-old girl getting her hair washed.

"Shit, these kids is grown now-a-days. You can't tell me she ain't never sucked a dick before," Delicious whispered.

"I'm done talking to you for the rest of the day." Mina shook her head. "Where is Mo? I thought she was coming in this morning."

"She running late too. You know she got all them badass kids over there. I swear if Boss shoot one more nut up in her, I'ma get my tubes tied for her."

"Don't talk about my godbabies. I'm happy for my friend. Just think, for years she couldn't have kids and now she's on her fourth baby."

"Ooh... just thinking about being pregnant with my fourth child makes my ovaries hurt," Delicious crouched over in agony.

"Whatever, she gives me hope." Mina choked up.

"Aww damn, that's right." Delicious slapped his hand against his thigh. "I am being so insensitive. Forgive me, it's that time of the month. How did the doctor's appointment go?"

"I'm not pregnant," Mina answered regrettably.

"Aww, boo, I'm sorry." Delicious wrapped his arms around her.

"It's ok," Mina shrugged, trying not to cry.

"I'll carry a baby for you." He rubbed her back.

"Stop, you gon' make me cry. My heart already feels like it got a fat chick sittin' on it," she chuckled.

"We're sorry, Mina." The other staff members said.

"It's gon' be alright. You gon' get pregnant, girl. Watch," Delicious declared.

"So, Delicious, you don't care about the fact you sleeping with a married man?" Mina's longtime nail technician, Neosha, asked.

"Look, until you've walked a day in a gay man's shoes, you straight fish will never understand what it's like to fear being shunned by your family for being gay. After I calmed down, Waymon explained everything to me. He cares for Selena but he was never in love with her. He had to do what he had to do in order to survive. I ain't mad at that. Besides, they getting a divorce now."

"Well, good luck with that, girlfriend, 'cause if he'll cheat on you once, please believe he'll do it again." Neosha gave him a word of warning.

"Don't you speak that word over my life, Satan." Delicious screwed up his face. "Waymon loves me. Ain't no way I'm giving up some bomb dick and a nigga wit' a job. I'm damn near 40. Who knows when I'm gon' luck up and find that again."

"Your priorities seem off," Janiya, a stylist, spoke up.

"God… Idris… the lotto… Waymon's penis. My priorities seem in check to me," Delicious snickered.

"And you foul as hell for being friends with that girl knowing you still fuckin' her husband," Neosha reminded him.

"Ex-husband," Delicious corrected her. "And Selena is moving back to Miami. I ain't never gotta see or hear from that broad again."

"You ain't shit," Mina giggled.

"I rebuke you, devil, in the name of Jesus." Jodie placed an invisible cross over her chest.

"You just mad 'cause you ain't gettin' no dick, dry coochie." Delicious stuck his tongue out at her.

Mina tried her hardest not to laugh but found it damn near impossible. She was laughing her ass off when the salon door swung open and in walked one of the finest men she'd ever seen. Her husband was by far the finest man on earth, but this young bull was giving Victor a run for his money. Mina didn't know who he was but he was a perfect work of art.

He had a bad boy, exotic swag about him that turned her the fuck on. He looked to be about 6'1, 215 pounds. He was 215 pounds of solid muscle. A white, Jordan snapback was cocked low on his head. You could still see his brows and almond-shaped eyes. The guy had the perfect nose and lickable lips. A thick, scruffy beard gave him an irresistible edge.

He wore a thin, gold, rope chain, a grey, oversized, holey Alexander Wang short-sleeve sweatshirt, fitted jeans and crisp, white, New Balance sneakers. The young boy was scrumptious; but what made him even sexier was the little girl's hand he was holding. All the ladies in the shop were swooning. Mina wasn't the type to be pressed over a dude but this guy had her going through changes. There was something about him that drew her to him. Foxy Brown's *Get Me Home* came to mind as she looked him in the eye.

"Hi, I'm Mina. How may I help you?" She extended her manicured hand for a shake.

"Bishop." He shook her hand and eyed her lustfully.

Bishop knew exactly who she was. Mina's name rang bells in the streets. Word around town was that she had the best salon in the Lou and was married to thee notorious Victor Gonzalez. But no one ever spoke about how bad she was. Bishop had seen a lot of fine-ass chicks in his short time on earth, but Mina was the sexiest woman he'd ever been blessed to see.

She wasn't too skinny or too thick. She was the perfect size. She had perky tits, a small waist, round hips, sumptuous thighs and a fat ass. The black Nirvana t-shirt and black over-the-knee boots emphasized her sex appeal. He'd never seen a woman make a t-shirt and boots look so fly. He had no business lusting after a married woman but Mina was the truth.

"So you're the famous Mina Gonzalez?" He continued to slowly shake her hand.

"I don't know about the famous part, but yeah, that's me," she blushed.

"That's what's up." He licked his bottom lip.

"You can let my hand go now," she laughed.

"Damn, my bad." He reluctantly let her go. "My niece got an appointment to get her hair braided wit' somebody name Delicious." He looked around.

"That would be me," Delicious waved. "You know I'm more than a beautician. I'm a barber too. You can always come sit in my chair." He flirted, swinging his leg from side to side.

"I'm good." Bishop shut down his advances.

"I'm just saying, you can pull up to my bumper, baby, wit yo' long black limousine," Delicious winked his eye.

"Delicious, stop!" Mina hit him on the arm. "You are making this boy uncomfortable."

"It's all good; but I'm a grown-ass man, ma. Ain't shit little about me." Bishop sucked his teeth, letting her know what was up.

"I bet it ain't, chile." Delicious fanned himself with his hand. "He so daddy! Yaaasssss I live!"

Mina looked at Bishop like he'd lost his mind.

"Settle down, sir, I'm a married woman." She flashed her ring.

"What ya man got to do with me? Shit... you keep eye-fuckin' a nigga and I might have to take you from yo' husband."

Mina furrowed her brows. *This li'l nigga got nerve,* she thought. But she liked his cocky attitude. He reminded her a lot of Victor when they were younger.

"You must not know who my husband is," she challenged.

"I know exactly who he is. I got mad respect for the OG, but it ain't my fault his wife diggin' the boy."

"How old are you?" Mina folded her arms across her chest and laughed.

"Old enough to put this pipe game down on you wit'out you being arrested." He flashed a dimpled grin.

"Girl, you betta stop flirting with this man before Yo Quiero Taco Bell come up in here and kill all of us." Delicious referred to Victor.

Delicious was right. Mina needed to stop while she was ahead.

"Okay, enough of that. No flirting. I do not have time for ruff, rugged and handsome in my life right now."

"But no, girl, is that a dimple? I could totally set up a tent in that dimple," Delicious sank his teeth into his bottom lip.

"I'd be naked in it." Mina unconsciously said out loud.

"See, I knew you liked me," Bishop smiled.

"No, I don't. I'm a grown-ass woman with kids, hot flashes and a mortgage. Their ain't nothing yo' little ass can do for me."

"I can think of a few things." His eyes traveled over her body.

Mina felt naked under his gaze.

"Is it just me or are you moist?" Delicious fanned his crotch.

It was time for Mina to walk away. The conversation was going left. She had no business flirting with another man. If Victor caught her, they'd both be dead. Bishop was young and still wet behind the ears. That didn't stop the wetness in her panties from building up. He'd activated something inside of her that hadn't been lit in years. Bishop was cute, but nothing or no one came before her husband.

"Let me stop playing with you. Delicious will get started on your niece's hair. You have a good day, Bishop." She grabbed her purse and switched extra hard to her office.

Halfway to her office, Mina gazed over her shoulder to see if he was watching her as she walked. He was watching. *You still got it, girl,* Mina smiled.

"My lonely ear, pressed against the wall of your words."

-Beyoncé, "Pray You Catch Me"

#5

"Fat mama!" Mina's dad, Ed, called her outside.

Mina slid off her parents' plastic-covered couch and rolled her eyes at the farting noise it made as she got up. She loved her mama and daddy to death but they were ghetto as hell. When her business started booming, she moved them out of Pagedale where she grew up and to the affluent Forest Park section of St. Louis. Businessmen, politicians and celebrities lived in the area. The houses ranged from one to five million dollars.

Mina thought when she moved them to the posh neighborhood that her mom and dad would class things up a bit. Well, Mina thought wrong. Their taste level remained at pig's feet and ramen noodles status. She was beyond embarrassed every time she visited. The outside of the house was painted doo-doo brown with the Louis Vuitton logo. In the front yard was a life-size statue of a black lawn jockey. He was smoking a blunt with his hands up, holding a sign that read: Don't Shoot. Several pink, plastic flamingos, a reindeer, Santa riding a slay, Christmas lights, and an old couch that her father sat on when he watered the lawn decorated the front yard.

If that wasn't bad enough, when you went inside the house, her mother, Rita, had the same couch set she had since Mina was five still wrapped in plastic. The tan and brown paisley print couch and loveseat were atrocious. The windows were covered with the ugliest pink curtains and drapes that had ever been made. A god awful, pink, ceramic vase filled with fake satin roses sat next to a floor model TV with aluminum foil on the antenna.

Mina didn't even know how the thing still worked. Her mother swore the TV made the living room look classy. Instead of going with updated hardwood or marble floors, her parents demanded that a salmon-colored carpet be put in.

The kitchen was even worse. Her parents refused to get it remodeled. They insisted that it be left just as it was. The kitchen had old pine wood cabinets and granite counter tops. Old-ass floral wallpaper lined the walls and the kitchen island. Her mom even had matching curtains on the backdoor and windows. An old fork and spoon set was nailed to the wall next to a picture of Jesus walking through the sand leaving his footprints behind. Fake, plastic apples, oranges and bananas sat in the center of the dining room table. Mina adored her parents but their over-the-top antics gave her a headache.

"Yes, Daddy?" Mina walked out to the side of the house where her father was barbecuing.

She immediately wanted to go back inside. Her father was outside barbecuing in a custom made, head-to-toe, fake Louis Vuitton logo suit. He had on a Louis Vuitton suit jacket, tie, slacks and dress shoes. What really almost gave Mina heart attack was the fact that he'd permed and pressed his hair. Her father now wore his shoulder length hair with a part on the side and flat ironed straight.

"You get you some of these ribs?"

"Daddy, you know I don't eat meat anymore." Mina eyed the ribs with disgust.

"You know damn well you ain't no fegan."

"A what?"

"Don't play with me. A fegan, girl!"

"It's vegan, Daddy. Vegan," Mina laughed.

"Fegan, vegan, frizzle, frazzle. It's all the same. Yo' body need meat, girl. It keeps you strong as an ox."

"Yeah, and when I ate meat I looked like an ox too," Mina challenged.

"Look at these muscles." Ed flexed his arm. "That's from these ribs."

"If you say so, Daddy." Mina massaged her forehead.

"Mina, you act like you was 'round here lookin' like Mama June. You looked good with that weight on you, babygirl."

"I was cute when I was a little thick'ums." She admired her frame.

"I don't care how much weight you lose. You always gon' by my fat mama." Ed hugged her from the side.

"Thank you, Daddy."

"Where is that big head husband of yours? I wanted to show him the new tool kit ya mama bought me for slanging that dick on her the other night."

Mina almost threw up.

"Daddy! Oh my God! I did not need to hear that." She felt herself become sick.

"Oh, girl, hush. How you think you got here?"

"Whatever, I think Victor's in the kitchen. I'll go get him." She walked back inside the house, flabbergasted.

Her whole family was in the kitchen. Mina's son, Lelah, Cousin Nay and her brother, Smokey, were at the table finishing dinner. Nay was showing Lelah her latest tattoo. Above her right titty was a tattoo of the McDonald's arch with a ribbon that said I'm Loving It. Mina wanted to slit her wrist. Nay was the epitome of ghetto fabulous. Meanwhile, Nay's 16-year-old son, Jimmy, Jr., acted like being there was the last place he wanted to be. Mina was low-key scared of him. He never talked. All he did was stare at you. He wore black eyeliner, black clothes, black nail polish and a bunch of silver jewelry.

Mina didn't know if he was a serial killer, vampire or a Goth kid. All she knew for sure, was that Jimmy, Jr. looked like he created bombs in his mother's basement. Nay's 14-year-old, pregnant daughter, Jaime, was in the middle of the kitchen floor showing her grandmother and Rita how to twerk. Jasmine, her third child, sat at the table watching YouTube videos with José. Nay's fourth child by her married, ex-boyfriend, Eric, lived with him and his wife. Her last two kids, Jareka and J. Cole, ran around the house like they didn't have any home training; which they didn't.

In the midst of all the chaos, Mina's Uncle Chester sat at the kitchen table asleep, snoring. His napkin was still stuck inside his shirt. Pieces of cornbread rested in the corner of his mouth. He looked like he couldn't breathe. His Sunday suit was so small the sleeves of his jacket squeezed his arms. It didn't matter the weather, Uncle Chester wore the same brown crushed-velvet suit from the 70's to church every Sunday.

"Aye! Aye! Aye!" Rita cheered Jaime on as she popped her booty.

"Y'all keep it up and she gon' go into labor." Mina said concerned.

Jaime was dancing so hard she'd begun to sweat. She acted like she wasn't even pregnant. Jaime knew how to twerk better than most strippers.

"You need to come over here and learn some of these dance moves. Shit like this will keep yo' man at home," Aunt Bernice exclaimed.

"Keep his dick hard," Rita cosigned.

"Ask yo' Uncle Chester. We stay gettin' it crackin'. Ain't that right, baby?" Aunt Bernice took a swig from her Crown Royal bottle.

When Uncle Chester didn't answer, Aunt Bernice called his name again.

"Chester!"

"Huh?" He snorted, waking up.

"I said ain't that right, baby?" Bernice said even louder.

Uncle Chester had a hard time hearing now.

"Ain't what right?" He looked around confused.

"You stay diggin' up in these guts, don't you, baby?"

"Mmm hmm." He nodded his head. "Shawty gotta big ole butt, oh yeah." He sang then went right back to sleep.

"See, Mina, you gotta learn how to ride that dick like a solider." Rita wound her hips in a circle.

"Show granny how to make my ass clap, Jaime." Aunt Bernice stood up straight and squeezed her butt cheeks one at a time.

Mina should've been used to her aunt and mom acting a fool, but she could never get used to seeing her almost 60-year-old, 5'11, 240-pound aunt dressed in a see-through, black cat suit and pleather, flat, knee-high boots shake her jelly. Her mother wasn't any better. She rocked a neon, printed cat suit with the back cut out and cut-outs on her butt cheeks. The red, cherry tattoo, dripping juices with her father's name written above it peeked through the cut-out on her butt. Rita's 16-inch, drawstring, burgundy ponytail was the icing on the cake. Mina wanted to gag and bound them both.

"Ma, did you really wear that to church?" Mina asked in disbelief.

"Yes, I wore a blazer over it to class it up a bit. What you mad?"

"Ma, you cannot wear a neon, cut-out cat suit to church. That's unholy and unsanitary."

"Why not? Jesus knows my heart."

"Y'all ain't gon' drive me to drink." Mina massaged her temples.

"Quit hating and turn the music up," Rita ordered.

Mina groaned and did as she was told. Future's *Freak Hoe* was playing.

"Awwwwwww yeah! That's my shit right there!" Rita bounced her butt to the trap beat.

"Oooh, girl, ain't he fine?" Aunt Bernice swooned over Future.

"Than a muthafucka. Nayvadius can get it. I would let him shoot up my club any day." Rita high-fived her sister.

"How in the hell Ciara gon' leave him and get wit' Russell Wilson Mr. Potato Head lookin' ass?" Aunt Bernice asked, placing her hand on her hip.

"I heard it was because he cheated on her while she was pregnant."

"Boo-hoo. All these niggas cheat. Well, except for my Chester."

"Girl, I knew that relationship was doomed as soon as she got them matching dreads," Rita cackled.

"Ciara better hope Russell ain't over there busting it wide open for a real nigga. That boy look like he keep a box of Fleet on deck."

"I have heard enough." Mina threw up her hands. "Where is my husband?"

She couldn't listen to one more minute of her mom and aunts' ridiculous conversation. They were starting to make her head hurt.

"He in the back somewhere." Rita swung her hair from side to side like she was Beyoncé.

Mina made her way to the back of the house where the bedrooms were. She stopped by her Nana Marie's door and peeked her head inside. She was sound asleep in bed. Nana Marie was the love of Mina's life. She was always there to love on Mina. She gave the best advice. Nana Marie was the calming force of the family. It hurt Mina to the core that she was mainly confined to her bed now.

Getting around wasn't so easy for her anymore. She needed help doing some of the most basic things like walking, eating, bathing and dressing herself. Her daughters, Rita and Bernice, were there every step of the way, taking care of her. Mina wished she could've been there more for her grandmother, but with her hectic schedule, she only got to see her once or twice a week.

"Mina, is that you?" Nana Marie said weakly.

"Yes." Mina walked all the way inside the room. "I thought you were sleep. I didn't want to wake you."

"I ain't seen you in a month of Sundays; you better come give an old woman a hug." Nana Marie reached out for her.

Even though time was doing a number on her physical abilities, she was still the prettiest woman Mina had ever seen. Nana Marie's long, gray, sponge-like hair was pulled back in a ponytail. Her brown eyes had lightened and almost looked gray. Age spots covered her face but Mina likened them to freckles. She'd lost so much weight that the veins in her hands protruded through her skin.

It tore Mina up to see her grandmother in such a delicate, feeble state. This was the same woman that used to scrub and mop rich white folks' homes just to feed and clothe her daughters. Nana Marie would work from sun up to sun down, ride the bus for several hours, clean her own home, fix dinner, take care of her girls, go to sleep and do the same thing all over again the next day. Mina had never met her grandfather. She didn't know much about him except for the fact that he left Nana Marie to raise their two girls alone. Rita and Bernice didn't even remember how their father looked. He was a mystery to them.

"Now you know I always come by to see my favorite girl in the whole wide world." Mina gave her grandmother a sweet kiss on the cheek. "You hungry? You wanna eat?"

"Naw, I know yo' daddy ain't did nothin' but burnt up the barbeque."

"He did," Mina chuckled. "Talkin' about it's Cajun."

"Chile," Nana Marie giggled. "Nana miss you."

"I miss you too, Nana."

"How you been?"

"Holding on, Nana. Holding on. The IVF treatment didn't work again."

"Oh, Mina, I'm sorry to hear that. I know how bad you wanted another baby. It'll happen, just watch. When you least expect it."

"I hope so," Mina replied solemnly. "I'm sorry, I haven't been by to visit as much as I used to. I just have so much going on."

"I understand."

"No, I feel bad. Since the shop will be closed Monday, I'ma come by and spend the whole day with you. We gon' watch Kelly and Michael, Days of Our Lives. We gon' do it big girl," Mina joked.

"I'd like that." Nana Marie smiled softly.

"You get you some rest now, you hear?"

"Yes, darling. I will."

"I'ma go find Victor. Love you, Nana." Mina gave her another kiss.

"I love you too."

Mina walked out of the room and gently closed the door behind her. She could hear Victor's voice from the spare bedroom, further down the hall. Mina stopped and stood by the door. His back was facing her. He was on the phone with someone talking in a hushed tone. She could barely make out what he was saying.

"Nah, I ain't gettin' out tonight. Gotta spend time with the fam…"

Mina cocked her head back and curled her upper lip. Why did Victor feel the need to dip off and have a private conversation alone? Straight men didn't whisper on the phone to each other so he had to be on the phone with a chick. *What the fuck is going on,* Mina wondered. Victor said he wasn't on no other shit but his actions weren't matching his words. Once again, instead of being with his family, he was off doing his own thing.

Mina immediately felt sick. All the signs were there. She couldn't deny it anymore. He was cheating on her. The question was: with who? Who was the woman taking up all her husband's time? It was taking everything in her not to lay down and die. She didn't want to lose her husband, but she would be damned if she was the only one participating in their marriage.

She tried to be blind to his ways but the nauseating ache in the pit of her stomach wouldn't allow it. He had a bitch on the side. Mina began to feel dizzy. What had she done to drive him away or had he just changed? She wanted to rush into the room and hit him with a barrage of questions, but what proof did she have besides her suspicions?

Mina would look jealous and crazy. But why did she need proof to confirm what her conscious already knew? Her spirit never steered her wrong. Some shit wasn't right. Victor was up to no good. She didn't want to believe that he could give his love away to another woman, especially when she'd been his number one cheerleader for the last 10 years.

She'd devoted herself to him and catered to his every need. He had no reason to seek any kind of assistance from another woman. Mina was all he should want or need.

"Mina!" Nay called out her name. "What you doing standing in the hallway?" She asked on her way to the bathroom.

Victor jumped and turned around and looked at his wife.

"Goddamnit Nay," Mina hissed, stomping her foot.

Now, Victor would know she'd been spying in on his conversation.

"Let me call you back." He ended the call abruptly.

Mina wearily went in the room.

"Who were you on the phone with?" She scowled.

"Nobody you know." He took her hand and made her sit on his lap.

Mina could taste the dishonesty all over his breath. *How did we get here,* she wondered. When did it become so easy for him to lie to her? In the past, Victor would've never been so callous and cold. Keeping her out of harm's way was always his goal. Now he was the one inflicting pain on her. He didn't even realize that with each lie, a part of her died. Mina no longer knew who her husband was anymore. This man before her was an imposter, a magician.

"You smell good." He held her close and sniffed her neck.

"What you mean nobody I know?" She quipped. "I know everybody you know."

"I was taking care of business."

"No, you on that bullshit. Let me find out you was on the phone with another bitch."

"Really, man? Fuck you talkin' about?" Victor eased her off his lap. "I'm here wit' you and yo' family and you accusing me of talkin' on the phone with somebody. What the fuck is wrong wit' you?" He squinted his eyes.

"You. You're what's wrong with me. You back here whispering on the phone and shit. Ain't no straight man whispering on the phone to no nigga. You think I'm stupid or something? You were on the phone with another girl."

"Here you go with that bullshit." Victor shot up. "You trippin'. I already told you what was up. Now you wanna keep pushing the issue? You gotta stop, man." He walked out and left her standing there.

Mina stood stone-faced. What was she to do? Ignoring the obvious wasn't an option anymore. She couldn't ignore, pray, drink or worry her suspicions away. She had to know for sure. Was he cheating on her?

Denial:

The action of declaring something to be untrue.

"What a wicked way to treat the girl that loves you."

-Beyoncé, "Hold Up"

#6

As promised by her husband, Mina was gifted with a full day at the Four Seasons Salon & Spa. With all of her erratic behavior lately, he demanded that she take a day to get pampered. She needed to relax her mind, body and soul. Mina lay in her big, white, fluffy robe trying to clear the troubling thoughts that crammed her head, but it was impossible. All she kept doing was replaying all the things she'd seen Victor do.

Flashes of him coming home late, hiding his phone and disappearing to have whispered conversation tormented her. It was all she could think about. She tried to erase the evidence that was building in her head, but she'd already convicted him as guilty. Mina had never been so sad in her life. This wasn't how she envisioned herself at the age of 36. This was supposed to be the happiest time of her life. She and Victor should've been in a groove. They were going into the second faze of their life.

But here she was, sulking, feeling worthless. Who was this bitch he was creeping with? *What does she have over me,* she thought. Whoever she was, she'd never love him the way Mina did. She knew Victor inside and out. The stairwell to his heart led to her; so why was he able to make her feel like she was invisible? It was like she was a ghost to him. He used to be able to pick up on her misery, now he was the cause of it.

Each day that passed felt like her last. She walked around floating on doubt and insecurity. Mina spent her days and nights fasting and praying to God to save her marriage. Instead of complaining and questioning him, she tried to change herself. Maybe if she was less awake the clues would dissolve. So, she wore her hair just the way he liked, cooked his favorite meals, became softer with her approach but nothing could stop the fear that grew inside her belly.

Paranoia consumed her. Any and everything he did she questioned. He'd already planted a seed of doubt in her. There was no stopping its growth. Mina tried to tell herself that everything she was feeling was unfounded. What if it was all in her head? What if she'd drove a wedge between them all on her own? What if she was going crazy? Was she on her Monica *So Gone* shit?

"What's wrong with you?" Mo, her best friend, turned and asked.

Mo's pink, 7 carat diamond engagement ring shined so bright it almost blinded Mina. After years together, she and the love of her life, Boss, were finally getting married. Mo was in the midst of planning her wedding. Mina hated to put a dark cloud over what should've been the happiest moment of Mo's life.

Mina was staring blankly off into the distance, on the verge of tears. Mo had kept her mouth shut, but for months she'd noticed that her friend wasn't the same. Mina was always on edge and in her own head. She seemed less sure of herself lately. The spark of light that used to flicker in her hazel eyes was no longer there. She was deteriorating right before Mo's eyes.

"Huh?" Mina came back to reality.

"What's going on?" Mo placed her hand on top of hers.

Mina gazed over at Mo's pregnant belly. How she wished she was carrying as well. Victor had moved on with life as if their failed attempt at IVF had never happened. He acted like he didn't care. He never once asked how she was coping with it all. Mina was starting to despise him and he didn't even know it. Sorrowfully, she looked up into Mo's eyes. They'd been friends since they met on the playground at the age of 10 years old.

Mo was more than her best friend. She was her sister before she knew she even had a real one. Mo was an absolute beauty. She was 5'9, with long, black hair, Godiva chocolate skin, doe-shaped eyes, high cheek bones and big, full lips. She had a modelesque body. The girl could eat whatever she wanted, have five million kids and not gain a pound.

They'd been through everything together: abusive boyfriends, being cheated on, miscarriages, broken hearts, kidnappings, the birth of their kids and more. Mo had gone through her fair share of heartache. Quan, her ex-fiancé, spent most of their relationship cheating on her. He even had a baby on her with a bird bitch named Sherry.

For years, Mina begged her to leave Quan's trifling-ass alone but Mo was determined to make their relationship work. Like most women, she thought if she stuck it out, she'd be able to change him. After nine years, four miscarriages, heated arguments and several knock-down, drag-out fights, Mo eventually used the common sense God blessed her with and moved on.

Now she was in a long-term, loving, healthy relationship with her children's father, Boss. They had three beautiful kids: a set of twin girls named Ryan and Makiah and a little boy named King. Mo and Boss were now working on their fourth child. She was six months pregnant with another boy. If Mina couldn't open up to anyone else, she could to Mo. They'd held each other down. Mo knew all of her deepest and darkest secrets. She held them all in a vault close to her chest. Mo would understand exactly where she was coming from.

"I think Victor is cheating on me." Mina finally confessed.

"Get the fuck outta here," Mo laughed, waving her off.

"No, I'm dead serious." Mina said with a straight face.

Mo eyed her to see if she would laugh or smile. When she didn't, she immediately went into comforting mood.

"Damn, for real? Not Victor." She replied, devastated. "I never thought I'd hear you say no shit like."

"Me either." Mina's heart broke into a million pieces.

"What makes you think he's cheating?"

"Ever since he came back, he's been acting hella weird. Like, his whole pattern has changed up. He's been coming home late at night, having secret conversations and shit—"

"Well, that don't necessarily mean he's cheating, friend," Mo chimed in.

"I know it don't, but, Mo, I know my husband. He's keeping something from me. I can feel it."

"Well, the one thing you can't deny is your female intuition. If you say something ain't right, it ain't right. Damn…" Mo inhaled deeply. "I never thought I'd be that chick that would be fighting and pregnant, but now I'ma have to fuck Victor up."

"If I don't give it to him first," Mina chuckled. "Peep game. We ain't even been fucking the way we used to. Victor used to stay on my ass. His dick used to get hard just by looking at me. We used to smash at least four or five days a week. Now weeks pass in-between us making love."

"That's all bad. Do you try to initiate with him or do you wait on him to come to you?"

"I mean, we ain't used to have to initiate nothing. It used to just pop off."

"Well, things change, friend. You gotta keep your sex life fresh. You can't slack off on that shit. You gotta make sure that nigga stay on it. You gotta keep him desiring you. So why don't you cop some lingerie and set up a li'l sexy night for y'all?"

"Fucking each other's brains out one night ain't gon' solve shit. The problem is still gon' be there. And why should I have to go to him? He's the one cheating on me—
"

"You wanna save your marriage, right?" Mo cut her off.

"Of course I do."

"Then you gotta do what you gotta do. You gotta sit that pride of yours aside. This ain't some regular nigga you talkin' about. This is your husband. If he is out here fuckin' around, you wanna dead that shit right now. You want him to remember what the fuck he got at home."

"Once again, why should I have to remind him of what the fuck he got at home? He should already know," Mina shot.

"'Cause niggas is stupid!" Mo exclaimed. "They dumb as hell. You know that. They do shit even though they know it's wrong. That's why we're here to remind them what's important and to put they ass back on track. It's a pain in the ass 'cause you basically playin' mama to your kids and your nigga, but when you love somebody, this is what you sign up for."

"Is it though or is that what we've been conditioned to believe?" Mina questioned. "I don't wanna have to babysit no grown-ass man. Victor's older than me. If he is dumb enough to risk our family for some new pussy, then I don't want him. I'm not gon' be fighting for a nigga's love. Fuck that. I ain't going through that shit again. Been there, done that, and I ain't doing it no more. Besides, sex ain't gon' solve everything. There is something big missing between us."

"Ok," Mo eased back in her seat and placed her cucumbers over her eyes. "Fuck around and let your pride cause you to lose your husband. Now I'm not advocating cheating, but Victor is a good man. If I was you, I'd give him one pass and try to save my marriage."

The night was winding down. Mina had just gotten out of the shower. The Guerlain citrus-scented shower gel had her feeling and smelling right. She lay snuggled underneath the covers in a fitted tank top and white boy shorts. The central air conditioner was on 63, so the house was nice cool. Sex and the City, the movie, was on the E network. Mina had seen the movie too many times to count but never got sick of it. The movie was all about the power of love. Mina's whole entire life was ruled by love.

After heavy contemplation, she decided to take Mo's advice. Her and Victor were in desperate need of a romantic night alone. All she had to do now was run it by him. Victor was a busy man so she couldn't just spring a surprise on him. Mina had to be penciled into her husband's schedule. Victor came out of the master bath fresh and clean for bed. His Dior Sauvage shower gel and body lotion heightened her senses.

The man smelled wonderful. Victor wore nothing but a new, clean pair of $145 HANRO soft-knit pajama joggers with no underwear underneath. The imprint of his dick reminded her of a thick kielbasa sausage. His smooth, well-built chest and biceps called her name. Mina adored her husband. Victor climbed into bed and lay next to her.

"Come here." He pulled her close.

Mina snuggled underneath his arm. It took everything in her not to lick his pec. She placed a soft kiss right by his underarm instead.

"You watchin' this shit again?" He asked not thrilled.

"Quit hatin'. You know it's one of my favorite movies of all-time." Mina played with the hair on his stomach leading to his happy trail.

"I swear, I know Big and Carrie life better than I know my own," Victor joked.

"Shut up," Mina laughed.

The movie was at the part where Carrie and Big lay in bed as she read to him from the book Love Letters of Great Men. While reading, Carrie stops to ask Big if he's ever written her a love letter. The question makes Mina wonder the same about her own man.

"Have you written me a love letter before?"

"No," Victor chuckled. "Do I look like the type of dude to write a love letter?"

"What?" Mina squealed. "You say that like it's a bad thing. I think it's very sweet. I would love if you did something like that for me."

"It's not my thing. I send you text messages tellin' you I love you every day."

"You do, but a text message and a love letter aren't the same," Mina disagreed. "A text message is so impersonal. A love letter is thoughtful. It shows how much time you put into your words, you know?"

"I guess." Victor tickled her forearm with his fingertips.

"I was thinkin'," Mina changed the subject. "This weekend we should have a romantic night for two. We need it. Don't you think?"

"That's cool. Just let me know what time and I'll be there." Victor kissed the top of her head. "Now turn this soft-ass movie off so we can go to bed."

"Know that I kept it sexy. Know that I kept it fun."

-Beyoncé, "Hold Up"

#7

"Take all of me. I just wanna be the girl you like. The kind of girl you like is right here with me." Mina sang as she placed the finishing touches on her barely-there outfit.

She swore to God that for better, for worse, for richer, for poorer, in sickness and in health to love and cherish Victor. Things weren't the best between them right now, but with some effort on her end, it could get better. She still stuck by her view that sex wouldn't solve everything, but it was a start.

Maybe if they were able to connect on a sexual level, everything else would fall back into place. Victor wasn't a bad guy. He'd been a phenomenal husband over the years. She hadn't had any problems out of him. He was damn near perfect. Mina held him up on a pedestal of excellence. She had to put her insecurities to the side and give Victor the benefit of the doubt.

It wouldn't be fair to him or their marriage if she didn't. All marriages had their ups and downs. Theirs was no different. Things wouldn't be rainbows and butterflies all the time. Right now they were experiencing their darker days. With time and determination on both their parts, they'd see brighter days again. To work their way back to greatest, they needed intimacy. Mina needed to know that her husband still found her desirable.

It fucked her up inside that he didn't ogle over her anymore. He used to make her feel like she was the prettiest, sexiest woman in the world. They used to talk to each other until the wee hours of the morning about their hopes and dreams, have impromptu dates, finish each other's sentences, but all of that seemed like a distant memory.

That night, everything would change. Mina had it all planned out. The kids were gone for a few hours so they had the house all to themselves. Victor was due to be home at 7:00 for dinner. What he didn't know was that she was dessert. Mina was going to ride his dick like it was a surfboard.

While cooking dinner, she'd already started pre-gaming. The D'Usse in her system had her feeling right. She couldn't keep her hands off herself. Mina was feeling herself to the 10th degree. Mo was right. Getting dolled up in sexy lingerie changed her whole attitude. There was something very empowering about looking like a sex kitten. It had been ages since she felt this alive.

Mina looked absolutely bewitching in an Agent Provocateur glittering, glimmering Azaleah – showgirl playsuit. The lingerie set exuded a coquettish charm at every turn. Inspired by the one and only Cher, the mesmerizing piece was formed of soft, flat bands of super-stretchy, black elastic adorned with triple rows of jet hematite Swarovski crystals that crisscrossed in flawless fashion across her form.

Hand-beaded, black, Swarovski tassel trim hung like tantalizing, shimmering curtains across the curves of her lower front torso, concealing and revealing for a thrillingly wanton finish. The rear was completely open. To complete the naughty look, she wore matching pasties and an eye mask. Her hair was filled with big, bouncy curls. Her makeup look consisted of black winged eye liner and a bold, red, matte lip.

Mina placed on her black Louboutin "So Kate" heels and sauntered down the steps. The sounds of Beyoncé's *Blow* thumped through the surround sound speakers. Mina danced to the hip 70's inspired beat. She couldn't wait till Victor got home so he could turn her cherry out. The mood for seduction was set. The lights were turned down low. The dining room table was set for two.

Five antique candle holders with white lit candles were strategically placed around a centerpiece of hot pink roses. A bottle of Ace of Spades chilled in a bucket of ice. That night they'd dine on their Hermes dinner plates. Mina only bought them out for special occasions. The food she'd prepared simmered on the stove on low. Before they devoured one another, they'd feast on lobster and steak.

Nervous butterflies filled the pit of her stomach. She couldn't wait until he laid eyes on her. Mina pulled out her cellphone and checked the time. It was a little after seven. Victor was late. Mina anxiously texted him.

<Messages   My Baby   Details

Where r u?

Victor quickly replied back: **on my way**. Happy that she would be seeing him soon, she put her phone down and took a deep breath. Two hours later, Mina sat at the table alone nursing her third glass of champagne. Pissed, she glared across the table at his empty seat. She wanted to break Victor's face. He hit her up twice saying he was coming but he still wasn't there. The disrespect on his end was unreal.

He knew how important this dinner was to her. Since when did he disregard her feelings and treat them like trash? Mina couldn't help but think he was with someone else. She didn't need to be slapped in the face with his infidelity. It was apparent that his heart was somewhere else. She often wondered when Victor was with her if he wished she was the other woman. Mina tried to be what he wanted her to be but it wasn't enough.

What was once her best was now mediocre at best. He didn't see her anymore. Someone else had his full attention. She just wished he'd let her know what was up instead of stringing her along. Her heart couldn't take anymore disappointment. It sucked that the only time she felt happy was when they were on good terms.

Thick, salty tears rolled down her face and neck. The saying that money can't buy your happiness was so true. There she was, in her 63-million-dollar mansion, while her husband was out doing God knows what and with whom. She felt like a fool sitting there half naked with nipple pasties and 5-inch heels on. Mina didn't know when love became elusive, all she knew was that she didn't have it. She was sick of wishing her husband would come home and pay her attention. Had he forgot that she was a bad muthafucka?

Mina checked her watch for the 100th time. It was almost ten o'clock. The kids would be back home any minute. Instead of texting him, Mina decided to give Victor a call. He had her completely fucked up. To her surprise, her call was forwarded to voicemail. Mina swore she'd been shot point-blank in the heart with an AK-47. A piercing silence swept over the room. *Who does this muthafucka think he is,* she wondered.

If he was trying to kill her, it was working. Every time he played her to the left, she died 100 times over. Distraught, she slowly rose to her feet and used what little energy she had to blow out the candles. This was the last straw. There would be no more trying on her part. She was done. Victor could kiss her narrow, black ass as far as she was concerned. If he thought he was going to get away with disrespecting her, Victor had another thing coming. Mina was going to put an end to all the bullshit that night.

Anger:

An intense emotional response. Often it indicates when one's basic boundaries are violated.

"Beautiful man, I'm the lion. Beautiful man, I know you're lying."

-Beyoncé, "Don't Hurt Yourself"

#8

Mina stood out on her bedroom balcony feeling like she wanted to throw up her insides. The blunt she smoked calmed her nerves some, but her hands wouldn't stop shaking as she dialed Victor's number for the 20th time. Each time she called, it was the same thing. The call went straight to voicemail. This time it was no different. This time, she decided to leave a message.

"Oh word? That's what we do now? It's fuck me, right? You really gon' sit up here and ignore my calls like I'm some bum bitch off the street? Nigga, fuck you! You got me fucked up. Whoever that bitch is you wit' you better stay wit' her ass tonight. 'Cause I'll be damn if you walk yo' black ass up in here tonight. Try me if you want to. I hate you!" She spat before hanging up.

Mina didn't know what type of game Victor was playing, but if he kept it up, he was going to lose his wife. She couldn't be a fool for him anymore. Never in a million years did she think he would ever put her in this kind of predicament. She had no idea who her husband had become. He swore he would shield her from any kind of hurt. He promised to never break her heart, lie or cheat. Now he was doing all three simultaneously. Mina couldn't continue to hold out hope that things would get better. By the second, it was getting worse.

She'd been here before. The feeling that her man was stepping out on her consumed her. It was just hard to believe that Victor would destroy her and everything they'd built. The man she married would never be so callous. Mina tapped her foot and tried to steady her rapidly beating heart as she called him again.

"Your call has been forwarded to an automatic voice system."

Mina held her head back and willed herself not to cry. Anger seethed through her veins. She hated Victor for doing this to her. Instead of fighting, they should've been making love until the sun came up. Victor had ruined everything now. There was no hope for them. Mina had lost all faith in him.

"Mom?" Lelah called out her name. "Where are you?"

Mina quickly put the blunt out, flicked it into the grass and spun around.

"Out here, baby." She fanned the air, praying to God that Lelah didn't smell the weed smoke.

Lelah stepped out onto the balcony. She quickly noticed that Mina had her hair up in a messy ponytail and was dressed in her ratty, old robe, t-shirt, dingy, oversized jogging pants and Ugg boots.

"What you doing out here?"

"Just getting some fresh air." Mina tried to play it cool.

"Mom, you been smoking that loud?" Lelah cocked her head to the side.

"That who?" Mina replied confused.

"That loud, that Kush, that KK?"

"Girl, speak English."

"Weed, mom, weed!" Lelah giggled.

"Absolutely not. I am a law abiding citizen."

"LIES! I can smell it all over you." Lelah sniffed her mom's shirt. "I'm tellin' Daddy."

"Good luck with that." Mina mumbled. "Y'all have fun at Dave & Busters?"

"Yeah; Jasmine, Jareka and J. Cole almost got us put out. They kept on stealing other kids' tickets."

"Oh Lord," Mina chuckled. "Where my baby at? He have fun?"

"Yeah, I wore his li'l butt out. He's taking a shower now so he can get ready to go to bed."

"Good."

"Where's Pop?" Lelah looked around. "I thought y'all were having a romantic dinner? When I left you were in here channeling your inner Beyoncé."

"I don't know where your dad is." Mina shrugged her shoulders.

She wasn't going to front like everything was all good.

"Mom," Lelah leaned up against the railing. "Is everything alright between you and my dad?"

"Why you ask that?"

"'Cause y'all have been arguing a lot lately. I know y'all think that we can't hear you but we can. José thinks y'all are gettin' a divorce."

Mina wanted to break down and cry. She never wanted her kids to worry about them.

"All couples fight but that doesn't mean we don't love each other or that we're gettin' a divorce. Are things a little tense between your dad and I; yes. But we'll be fine. You guys have nothing to worry about." Mina tried to convince Lelah and herself.

"Good," Lelah smiled. "Now I don't have to worry about which parent I would go live with if y'all got a divorce," she laughed.

"Girl, hush, you about to go off to school and have your own place soon; but if it came down to it, it would be me of course," Mina giggled.

"I told José y'all were ok. I figured y'all were doing the nasty or something. 'Cause I tried calling Pop twice but he ain't answer."

Panic raced through Mina's body. It was one thing for Victor not to answer her calls, but he would never ignore the kids. Something had to be wrong. *Oh my God, what if he's hurt? What if he got in an accident on the way home,* Mina's mind began to race. She felt like a total idiot for not thinking that his life could be in jeopardy. Victor had been stressing how his biggest worry was not coming home to her. Mina would never forgive herself if one of his rivals had gotten to him and the last words she said to him was fuck you, I hate you.

"I gotta go. Watch your brother. I'll be right back." Mina raced inside the house.

"What's wrong?" Lelah asked, seeing the panic on her mother's face.

"Nothing, I'm about to go check on your dad."

"Is everything ok?"

"Yeah," Mina lied, grabbing her black, Prada leather city saddle bag and car keys. "Just keep an eye on your brother." She rushed down the steps and out the door.

Fifteen minutes later, Mina pulled up in front of Victor's new club. She hadn't been there since the grand opening. 1108 was the hottest new club in St. Louis. It was located in the heart of the city in an abandoned warehouse. Victor had totally transformed the place. It went from being nothing but bricks and rubble to a three-story club that celebrities like Floyd Mayweather, Diddy, Lala and Carmelo Anthony frequented.

It was Saturday night so there was a line around the corner for people to get inside. Two bouncers and a security guard stood at the front entrance door. Mina looked to see if she saw Victor's car parked outside. There was a line of luxury cars parked out front but none of them were his. This caused Mina to panic even more. The fact that she didn't see his car made her fear the worse.

Mina turned the engine off and hopped out the car. She needed answers and quick. There was only one person that would be able to give them to her. Victor's longtime employee, Julisa. If there was anyone that knew where he was, it was her. The music from inside the club was so loud it caused the ground to shake. Mina could feel the bass as she walked. When she approached the doors, the bouncers and security guard recognized her face and stood at attention.

"Mrs. Gonzalez, it's nice to see you again." One of the bouncers said nervously.

"Hi." Mina gave them all a friendly smile, although she was worried sick over her husband.

"Is there anything we can help you with?" Tony, the security guard blocked her path.

"No, thank you." Mina gave him a look that said move.

Tony caught the hint and reluctantly stepped to the side. Mina could've easily asked one of them if they'd seen Victor but she didn't want the staff in their business. It was bad enough that she looked like a crazed wife popping up at the club trying to find her husband. Her hair nor makeup was done and she had on a robe and Ugg boots for God sake. The sight wasn't pretty. Normally, Mina wouldn't have been caught dead in such a getup, but questions needed to be answered. Her husband could've been laid out in a ditch somewhere. She didn't give a fuck how she looked.

Mina entered 1108 and took it all in. Victor had worked himself to the bone to create a posh environment. The 3,500-square-foot space seduced you upon entry. The modern décor was highlighted with bronzed architecture, gold-flecked table tops with dark, wooden accents and of course stripper poles. These poles weren't for topless dancers but for some of the sexiest go-go dancers in town.

It was darkly lit inside, which made the clubbers feel uninhibited. Frantically, Mina walked around searching for a face she knew. People were looking at her like she was crazy. Mina blocked out the stares and stayed focused. She had to find out what was going on with her husband. Finally, she spotted Julisa behind the bar talking to a bartender.

"Julisa!" She yelled over the loud music.

"Mina?" Julisa's eyes grew wide.

She was surprised to see her there. Mina never came to the club. She was especially shocked to see her there looking so disheveled. Mina looked like she hadn't slept in weeks. Julisa stepped from behind the bar and gave her a warm hug.

"How are you? Is everything ok?"

"No, umm," Mina looked around anxiously. "Have you seen my husband?"

Julisa swallowed hard and held Mina at arm's length.

"He umm… just left a little while ago. He said he was on his way home."

"How long ago was that?"

"About… maybe 20, 30 minutes ago."

"Ok." Mina replied speechless.

She didn't know what to do. Victor was either at home by now or in trouble. Mina pulled her phone out her purse and tried calling him again. Her call went to voicemail once more. *Lord, let him be ok,* she prayed.

"If you hear from him, tell him I'm looking for him and to call me immediately," she ordered.

"Yes, sure, of course," Julisa guaranteed.

She noticed how panic-stricken Mina was. She felt terrible for her.

"You have a goodnight." Mina's voice cracked.

She was trying to keep it together, but the thought of Victor not coming home to her nearly killed her. She didn't know what she would do if she ever lost him. Disoriented, Mina left out the backdoor exit. The warm night air hit her smack dab in the face. It was hot as hell outside; but even with all of the out-of-season clothes she had on, Mina felt cold. If she returned home and Victor wasn't there, she'd lose her shit for sure.

How would she call his mother and tell her that her son was either dead or missing? His mother, Faith, had been through enough. She'd been in Mina's shoes. She understood what it was like to be married to a drug kingpin. She'd done it for years. She knew all about the sleepless nights, threats, police surveillance and bitches plotting to take your man. Mina didn't want to worry Faith, but the longer she was unable to get in contact with Victor, the more it looked like something bad had happen. Mina was just about to turn the corner and head back out front when out of the corner of her eye she spotted Victor's car parked against the fence.

"The fuck?" She stopped dead in her tracks.

Julisa had said he'd just left. *Why is his car here,* Mina scrunched up her forehead. All of the anxiety and fear she felt disappeared and was replaced with rage. She was being played for a fool.

"I'ma kill him!" She pulled the door open and stormed back inside.

Fire scorched through her veins. Mina stood in the center of the dance floor. Her eyes darted from left to right. Victor was there. She could feel his presence in the room. For his sake, it was safer that he not be there, 'cause when

Mina got a hold of him, it was curtains. She didn't see him anywhere. Then it dawned on her. *He's in his office.* Mina looked up at the third floor. His curtains were closed but the light was on.

"Muthafucka," she snapped, taking off running.

Julisa spotted a woman sprinting through the crowd like a mad woman. She was about to call security when she realized it was Mina. She'd watched her leave out but she was back.

"Fuck!" She dashed through the sea of people to get to her. "Mina, stop! You can't go in there!"

Mina heard her but kept running. How the fuck was she going to tell her she couldn't go into her husband's office? Nothing or no one was going to stop her from learning the truth. Julisa tried to catch up to her but Mina was too fast. Plus, she had on Ugg boots, whereas Julisa wore heels. Mina took the steps two at a time.

The bottom of her robe flapped behind her. Anger gave her the adrenaline rush she needed. Before she knew it, she was at Victor's office door. Mina placed her hand on the knob and turned. She didn't know what she expected to see when she walked in, but the visual before her nearly took her out at the knees.

There her beautiful husband was sitting at his desk while some Evelyn Lozada-lookin' bitch kissed him on the lips. All of the air in Mina's lungs vanished. She knew he was lying. Her biggest fear was coming true. Victor was cheating on her.

"Mina, I'm sorry." Julisa panted, standing behind her.

Victor turned and looked at her. He quickly pushed the unknown woman away and stood up.

"Baby, it's not what you think." He tried to explain.

"I've been callin' you all night and you haven't bothered to answer once. Now I know why." Mina tried to hold it together.

"What are you talkin' about? I didn't even know my phone was off." Victor looked down at his phone.

Sure enough, his phone was off.

"Did you touch my phone?" He asked the woman.

"No," she lied.

The chick had turned his phone off. Victor rushed over to Mina who stood paralyzed. He'd done it. He'd officially killed her. On June 20th at 11: 20pm, they'd tell the coroner that she'd died from heart failure.

"Baby, talk to me." Victor shook her arms. "I swear to God it's not what you think."

"It's not what I think?" Mina came to. "I walk into your office and see you kissing another bitch, but it's not what I think?" She pushed him off her.

"What the fuck is it then, Victor? Who is this bitch?" She pointed.

The woman walked from behind his desk with a calculated look on her face and said, "I'm Samia. Lelah's mother and his wife."

"I don't want to lose my pride but I'ma fuck me up a bitch."

-Beyoncé, "Hold Up"

#9

"What?" Mina said in disbelief. "Victor, who the fuck is this bitch?"

"I'm his wife," Samia repeated herself.

"Bitch… bye," Mina looked at her like she was stupid. "Now, I don't know what type of sick-ass game you two are playin' but unless you Jesus, bitch, Lelah's mother is dead!"

"Mina, she's telling the truth," Victor verified.

"What?" Mina stepped back and glared at the woman.

The chick did look like an older, sexier version of Lelah. Mina tried to deny her beauty but the bitch was drop-dead gorgeous. She had long, silky, brown hair with honey blonde highlights, smooth, butter-colored skin, cat-shaped eyes, picture-perfect lips and cheekbones so high they'd cut a bitch. Her body was on another level. Mina thought her body was banging but this chick's body took the cake. Her 38D breast implants sat firm inside the sheer body suit and blazer she wore. The leather leggings she rocked clung to her thick thighs and bountiful ass. The girl looked like she stayed in the gym.

Mina couldn't help but notice that the chick had somewhat of a smirk on her face. Mina didn't know what the fuck the bitch found funny. Maybe it was her outfit? Mina did look a hot, crusty mess. She hated that the first time she came in contact with Victor's side piece she was looking like a hobo. The fact that she wasn't beat to capacity and slaying a designer outfit was the least of her worries though. She had to A) Find out if this woman was really Samia and B) find out why the fuck she was kissing her husband.

"Remember I told you that I had some shit I was dealing with that you couldn't comprehend?" Victor asked.

"Yeah." Mina nodded, confused.

"This was it."

"I don't understand. You said that Samia was dead."

"That's what I thought. Until one day I was sent an anonymous email that said, "is this your wife" with a picture of Samia attached. When I saw the picture, I couldn't believe my eyes. There Samia was walking down the street healthy and alive. I thought the picture was photoshopped but it was real, so I went to Columbia to find out more information."

"When?" Mina asked clueless. "'Cause me and you ain't never been to no damn Columbia. You always said it was too dangerous to go back."

"It is. That's why I went by myself. When I went away for six months, I was actually in Columbia trying to find Samia," he explained.

Before Mina knew it, she'd reared her hand back so far, she slapped fives with Whitney Houston and then smacked Victor so hard his lip began to bleed.

"You did what?" She hit him repeatedly in the face.

Victor tried blocking the hits to no avail.

"Mrs. Gonzalez, stop!" Julisa jumped in. "Mr. Gonzalez, do you need me to call security?"

"Bitch, I wish you would!" Mina focused her wrath on her. "After everything I've done for you, you gon' have the audacity to ask my husband some shit like that? Bitch, if it wasn't for me, you wouldn't have this job. I should slap the shit out yo' ass too." She reared her hand back to hit Julisa.

"Parada, Mina! Cálmese! Esto no tiene nada que ver con ella!" Victor yelled in Spanish.

"English, nigga! Speak English! You know I don't understand what the fuck you saying!"

"I said, calm the fuck down! This ain't got shit to do with Julisa! This is between you and I! I caused all of this but I can explain."

"Explain what? That you left me and your kids for six months without any form of communication so you can go play a game of Where's Waldo with this bitch?" She pointed at Samia. "I should slap yo' ass again!" Mina tried to hit him.

"Yo!" Victor ducked and dodged the hit. "I understand that you're mad, but don't put your hands on me no more. That ain't even how me and you get down."

"That ain't even how we get down? Muthafucka, do you hear yourself right now? You sound stupid!" Mina slapped him in the back of his head.

Tired of her hitting him, Victor swiftly grabbed her by the arms and slammed her down onto the couch.

"I told you to stop fuckin' hittin' me!" He yelled.

"I'ma let you handle this. I'll be outside." Samia slowly sashayed out of the room.

"Yeah, you do that!" Mina tried to get up so she could hit her too.

"Stop!" Victor placed all of his weight on top of her.

"No, you stop! You lied to me! You had me sitting up here stressed the fuck out for six whole months not knowing if you were alive or dead. Hell, I didn't even know if you were coming back. You know how many nights José cried for you? Lelah worried herself sick and you see what happened to me." She flared her nostrils.

"I'm thinkin' you about to go to jail, but nooooo, you off in Columbia playing Captain Save a Ho." She mean-mugged him. "So all that shit about the feds being after you was a lie?"

Victor sat quiet. He knew that if he answered it would only make the situation worse.

"Answer the fuckin' question, Victor, and you bet not lie!" Mina fumed. "Did you lie about the federal investigation?"

"Yeah." He held his head down, ashamed.

Mina chuckled.

"I can't believe this shit. I fuckin' hate you." She began to cry.

Tears rolled out of the corner of her eyes and landed on the leather cushion.

"I couldn't tell you the truth 'cause I didn't know if she was alive for real or not. I didn't know if the Saldono Nation were still after her, and if they were, I didn't want them coming after you too. This whole thing was very dangerous. I had to keep everything on the low until I gathered all the information."

"So it took you six months to find this bitch?" Mina scowled.

"No, the reason it took me so long to come back was because I had to pull a few strings to get Samia a visa so she could enter the states."

"What kind of visa? A working visa?"

"No… she has an Immigrant Visa 'cause… she's… my wife." Victor braced himself for the blow.

Mina heard his words but refused to let it register in her brain. If Samia was alive, that meant that Mina and Victor's marriage was null and void.

"Get the fuck off me!" She tried with all her might to push him away.

"No! I'm not lettin' you go!"

"How could you do this to me?" Mina cried so hard her lungs became sore.

"Baby, I'm sorry." Victor cried too.

This was the moment he'd been avoiding since he returned. He knew once Mina learned the truth, their whole marriage would go up in flames. There was no way that he could tell her that Samia was alive and that their marriage wasn't real in the eyes of the law.

"Victor, get off of me! GET OFF OF ME!" She kicked and screamed on the verge of a mental breakdown.

"No! I told you I'm never lettin' you go!"

"Get off of me!" Mina bit the side of his face, leaving a mark.

Victor jerked back, stunned. He wanted to slap the shit outta Mina but quickly remembered he didn't hit girls and Mina was his wife. The minute he jumped back, Mina pushed him with all her might and ran out of the office in a heap of tears. There would be no more talking. Mina had heard enough of his bullshit that night. Victor had placed his line in the sand. Mina took all of his lies and secrets as a declaration of war. He'd blown up what little sanity she had left. It was time to fuck his world up.

"Tonight I'm fuckin' up all yo' shit, boy."

-Beyoncé, "Don't Hurt Yourself"

#10

Mina stormed past the security guards outside her home and unlocked the door. As soon as she stepped inside, she gasped and fell down on her knees. The whole car ride home, she'd willed herself not to cry. Holding back her tears felt like she'd died from drowning. Finally, able to breathe, Mina let out a blood-curdling cry that was so loud she woke Lelah. Her whole, entire world had been turned upside down and there was nothing she could do about it. Everything she thought to be true was a lie.

The man she'd loved her whole, entire life belonged to another. How would Mina ever be able to compete with a bitch that had literally come back from the dead? Samia was his first love, the mother of his firstborn child. If she'd never been declared dead, they would've still been together. There would be no Mina and Victor. Mina sat on her knees hunched over, barely able to breathe.

"Mom! What's wrong?" Lelah came racing down the steps. "Is Pop ok? Please don't tell me he's dead."

As much as her parents tried to shield her and José from their father's career choice, Lelah knew exactly what he did for a living. Everyone knew who her father was. There was no getting around the fact that they had security cameras all over the house and armed gunman outside their door. Lelah knew she came from the Gonzalez drug cartel. She knew that their family was public enemy number one.

Mina wanted to calm Lelah's fears but the pain she was experiencing was too excruciating to formulate words. Ever since she and Victor said I do, they'd lived a picture-perfect life. They were like Barbie and Ken, Barack and Michelle, Jay Z and Beyoncé. You couldn't tell her that they wouldn't live happily ever after. When she needed him most, he rode up on his white horse and saved her from the evil dragon that was Andrew.

For years they never cursed, screamed or lied. Mina and Victor were the definition of a real-life Disney movie. They were the couple that other couples wished they could be. Nothing could burst their bubble. Mina thought they were indestructible. She thought their love would stand the test of time but God had a funny way of shaking up shit. They no longer lived in paradise. The wicked witch had come and blew their house down. Mina had bit the poison apple and was sentenced to die. Unlike Samia, she wouldn't be resurrected. She was left out in the wilderness. No royal kiss could save her. Mina's fantasy was over.

All the things she thought she knew were untrue. Victor had hidden a secret from her so big that she would never be able to trust him. For months he sat back and watched her fall. With each day that passed and he treated her indifferent, a piece of her chipped away. He could've stopped it but he didn't.

"Mom! What's wrong?" Lelah shook her profusely. "Is Pop ok?"

"Why are y'all yelling?" José stood at the top of the stairs, rubbing his eyes, dressed in his Spiderman pajamas.

"José, go back to bed!" Lelah demanded, holding Mina in her arms.

José focused in on his mother. He never saw her so distraught in his life. Tears the size of lemon drops fell from her eyes.

"What's wrong with Mom?" He eased closer, afraid of what her answer might be.

"Take yo' ass back upstairs!" Lelah pushed him back, almost causing him to fall.

"No! What's wrong, Mom?" José slapped her hand away. "Mom, are you ok? What's wrong?" He teared up.

José often gave Mina a hard time but he loved his mom more than the air he breathed. Seeing his mom such a mess tore him up inside. Mina didn't mean to make her kids cry, but she couldn't stop the tears that traveled up her spine, through her throat and out of her eyes. All she kept thinking was that her intuition was right. She didn't want it to be true, but Mina wasn't the silly girl she used to be.

She'd learned to trust her instincts. She knew a cheating-ass-nigga like the back of her hand. She tried to convince herself that it was all in her mind but Victor had switched up his whole routine. It was beyond her how he thought she wouldn't peep game.

"Mom! Answer me! What is going on?" Lelah begged.

Mina was just about to respond when Victor burst through the door. He'd done 90 on the highway to get to her. Saving whatever was left of their marriage was his main priority. Victor walked in and saw Mina sprawled out on the floor with his children surrounding her. He'd never felt like a bigger piece of shit.

"Oh mi Dios . Gracias al Señor. You're alright." Lelah sighed with a sense of relief.

Now that she knew her father was ok, the question still remained, what was wrong with her mom? As if she'd been activated for war, Mina shot up from the floor and wiped her face with the back of her hand. She'd be damned if she let him see her cry. Mina shot Victor a deadly glare. He stared back at her. He didn't know if she was going to run at him or what. For the first time, he didn't know what his wife was thinking.

"Mina, let me talk to you," Victor pleaded with his eyes.

Mina looked at her husband. Even in the midst of her anger, the beauty of Victor was still evident. His strong gaze held her captive. He was beautiful. His smooth beard, mouthwatering lips and broad shoulders filled the room. How would she ever be able to leave him? He was all she knew. He was her man and she was his girl.

"GET OUT!" Mina's voice cracked as she screamed.

"Nah, you gon' let me talk to you!"

"I ain't gotta do shit but stay black, pay my taxes and die!" Mina quipped.

"Why are y'all fighting?" José asked frightened.

"Cause your father is a low-down, dirty, sack of shit! That's why we're fighting! Do you know what you've done to me?" Mina's hazel eyes darkened. "You have ruined me."

"If I could do things differently, I would," Victor tried taking her hand.

"Don't touch me," Mina snatched her hand away. "You will never touch me again. It's so over between me and you it ain't even funny." Her voice shook.

"Don't say that. You don't mean that."

"The hell I don't. You lied to me. Me!" She pointed to her chest. "You could've told me what was up. I would've been there for you. But you didn't 'cause you still love her, don't you?" Mina's eyes clouded with tears.

Victor stood silent.

"Answer the fuckin' question!"

"What the fuck is me answering that gon' solve?" He challenged.

"It's gon' solve whether you live or die tonight. Now answer the fuckin' question. Do you still love her?"

Victor clenched his jaw and looked away. There was no way on God's green earth he was going to answer that question.

"It's all good," Mina sucked her teeth. "You ain't gotta answer. I don't give a fuck if you do or you don't." She inhaled deeply.

"Did you fuck her?"

"Can we go upstairs? I'm not talkin' about this with you in front of the kids."

"Why not? They deserve to know they daddy ain't shit."

"That's not fair," Victor replied, feeling like he'd been spit on.

"Fair… fair?" Mina rolled her neck. "You the last muthafucka to ever talk about fair, when you been hiding this bitch from me for months. So be a man. Answer the question. Did… you… fuck… her?" She slapped her hands together with each word.

"YEAH!" Victor threw his hands up in the air. "One time. That make you feel better?"

Mina held her breath and willed her knees not to buckle. Her body felt as if it was going into epileptic shock. She figured they'd slept together but still had convinced herself that his response would be no. Without saying another word, she turned and made her way up the steps.

"Where you going?" Victor asked, afraid of what she might do.

Mina ignored his question and kept walking. The spirit of Angela Bassett in *What's Love Got To Do With It* had invaded her body. She didn't know who Victor thought she was but he had her completely, utterly fucked up. Unconsciously, Mina entered his walk-in closet and began to tear his clothes off the hangers one-by-one. Race-walking, she took the clothes and threw them across the balcony. Victor's clothes floated to the floor like feathers.

"WHO THE FUCK DO YOU THINK I AM?" Mina shouted causing spit to fly out of her mouth.

"What you doing? Put my fuckin' clothes back!" Victor said angrily.

Mina tossed his shoes, diamond jewelry, suits and ties over the balcony, furiously.

"I ain't puttin' shit back! You gettin' the fuck outta here tonight!" She grabbed a pair of scissors and went to work on his designer jeans. "You think you gon' lie to me for months and it's gon' be alright? You think you gon' cheat on me and I'm just gon' be like ok? I'm Mina fuckin' Matthews, nigga! I ain't no average bitch, boy! You know how many niggas I've curved on the strength of you? I could've been out here fuckin', but nah, here I am stuck on stupid, loving you!" She threw the cut up pieces of clothes on the floor.

"She's your wife, right?" Mina eyed him over the balcony. "Go live with that bitch! Go ruin her life!"

"Dad, what is she talkin' about? Do we need to call a doctor or something?" Lelah feared for her mother's sanity.

"Nah, baby, yo' mama ain't crazy. Yo' daddy just got life fucked up. You wanna tell 'em, Victor?" Mina challenged. "Tell them why we're fighting. Tell'em why we about to get a divorce."

"I'm not tellin' them like this. No," he refused.

"Why not? Tell 'em, big homey. You the OG, right? You ain't scared of shit. Tell 'em what yo' lyin'-ass been up to."

"I don't wanna know." Lelah shook her head.

"Ohhhh… yes you do." Mina nodded her head.

"Mina, stop!" Victor shot her a look that could kill.

"Nah, nigga, you wanted to be around here lying and fuckin' around! Tell 'em the truth! Tell 'em they daddy ain't shit!"

"Pop, what did you do?" José asked, holding onto his sister.

"Nothin', man. Me and your mom just going through something right now."

"There you go lyin' again!" Mina slapped her hand against her thigh. "You just don't know when to stop! Either tell them the truth or get out!"

"Mina, don't do this—"

"Don't do what? She deserves to know the truth."

"Who deserves to know the truth?" Lelah eyed her parents, confused.

"You, honey, you deserve to know the truth. It's the least your father can do since he didn't feel I deserved the decency of knowing what he's been up to."

Victor didn't know what to do. All eyes were on him. Mina was right; he wasn't scared of much. He'd stared a man in the eye and killed him without flinching, but the thought of telling his baby girl that her mother wasn't dead, terrified him to the core.

"If you don't tell her, I swear to God I will," Mina warned.

Victor hung his head low then looked his daughter square in the eyes.

"Your mother… your real mother." He looked up at Mina then back at Lelah. "She's alive."

"So what are you gonna say at my funeral, now that you've killed me?" – Beyoncé (Lemonade)

#11

A few days had passed by, but for Mina, it seemed like an eternity. She was stuck frozen in time. Anger and hurt consumed her. Victor had killed her without a knife or a gun. His lies and infidelity caused her to bleed internally. On her gravestone would read: Here lies the mother of my children who I took for granted and shroud in loneliness.

Mina inhaled the smoke from the Benson and Hedges cigarette in her hand and gazed out the kitchen window. She wasn't much of a cigarette smoker, but her nerves were so bad it was the only thing that calmed her down, besides poppin' a Xanax. Mina hadn't combed her hair or slept in days. Her favorite robe covered the pink and black negligee she wore. She was no longer a fully-functional human being. She tried to put on a strong face but Victor had turned her from a woman of substance to a coldhearted, angry, black bitch. Mina maneuvered through the house like a robot. Endless bottles of wine was her only form of nourishment.

Mina watched as José played in the yard. He'd gone on with life the best he could. Mina would catch him feeling blue but he'd always perk up as soon as he saw her watching him. He wanted to be a big boy for his mother. José didn't want her to have to worry about him too.

Lelah, on the other hand, was in a complete state of shock. She couldn't believe that after years of living her life without her biological mother, Samia was alive and ready to have a relationship with her. Lelah tried to hide her excitement for Mina's sake, but Mina could see that she was eager to meet her mom. The Christian side of Mina was happy that Lelah had the opportunity to build a relationship with her.

Every young girl deserved to have their birth mom in their life. She deserved to learn where she got certain traits and characteristics from. The selfish side of Mina wanted to scream and shout, "But what about me? I'm your mom! I raised you! Fuck that bitch!" No one could understand the pain she was enduring. Her family was being snatched right from underneath her and there was nothing she could do about it.

In a matter of days, she'd lost everything. Her man, whom she loved with every fiber of her being, was technically not her husband. Her daughter was being reclaimed by her biological mother. All she had left was

José and her salons. Instead of hiding out in the house, Mina should've been enjoying her summer. Everyone knew summer was the perfect time for love. She and Victor should've been dancing under the light of the moon instead of beefing.

After their big blow up, he'd taken her warning and left. Although she hated his guts, she waited by the phone each day for his phone call. She wanted him to fight for her, but he didn't. He called the kids to check on them but he hadn't uttered a word to her since he walked out the door. Mina just knew he would've bombarded her with a million reasons why she should forgive him. She for damn sure had a 100 million reasons why she should walk away.

Their entire relationship was fake. What they shared wasn't love. It was the perfect illusion. He'd tricked her into believing he was her knight in shining armor. When in reality, he was a wolf in sheep's clothing.

"Excuse me, Mrs. Gonzalez." Rosario the maid got her attention.

Mina wearily turned and looked at her.

"It's Ms. Matthews now." She corrected her.

"I'm sorry. Ms. Matthews, you have a visitor."

Mina gestured for whoever it was to come in.

"Girl, you better get them damn security guards together. They act like they ain't even wanna let me in." Mo wobbled into the kitchen.

She looked so cute pregnant. Her stomach protruded through her black bodycon dress. Mo was all stomach. She hadn't gained an ounce of weight anywhere else. The only way people knew she was pregnant was when she turned to the side. Mo stopped dead in her tracks and looked Mina up and down with disgust.

"Ok, friend, I know you over here going through it. Lord knows I do, but you need to pull it together. It's two o'clock in the damn afternoon and you still got your robe on." She placed her hand on her hip.

"So… a robe is just a long coat made of towel," Mina said, simply.

"You're a mess." Mo placed her Birkin bag on the table and sat down.

Mina's kitchen was flawless. It had an industrial flair to it, yet it was warm and cozy. The walls were pure white. The cabinets and kitchen island was made out of distressed wood. The countertops were made out of the finest Italian marble. Two large, industrial lights lit up the space. Instead of having a traditional dining table, she had a concrete, extendable one designed that cost $8,000. On one side of the table was a crème love seat with pillows, and on the other, two wicker chairs. A rectangle-shaped, sky blue, rustic planter box with three vintage mason jars and fresh flowers was the centerpiece.

"I'll take that." Mo took the cigarette from Mina's hand and put it out in the ashtray.

"I was smoking that."

"Now you're not. My baby not about to have secondhand smoke because you over here thinkin' you Bernadine."

"Fuck you," Mina laughed. "Didn't nobody ask you to come over here and bother me. I'm enjoying my misery just fine."

"I can't tell. I saw the way your eyes lit up when I walked in here. You missed me, bitch. You know you need me right now."

"Whatever, get over yourself."

"For real. How you feel?" Mo asked concerned.

"Like shit." Mina answered, honestly.

"I can't believe that bitch is alive and that Victor knew this whole time. You called it. You said something was going on. I just never thought Victor would do some shit like this."

"That makes two of us." Mina rolled her eyes.

"I know Lelah is all over the place."

"She is. We all are."

"I'm sorry this is happening to you." Mo rubbed her arm. "I don't know what I would do if I was in your shoes right now. I'm surprised you ain't on suicide watch."

"Trust me, I'm barely holding on."

"So what are you gonna do?"

"I don't know. I'm still in shock over everything. I don't even know what day it is. If it wasn't for the kids, I honestly would end it all."

"Don't talk like that," Mo scolded her.

"I'm dead serious, Mo. My whole life has vanished before my eyes. How do I recover from this? I don't even know where to begin."

"Have you talked to Victor? How does he feel about all of this?"

"I don't know and I don't give a fuck.," Mina shrugged her shoulders dismissively. "Victor can kiss my ass for all I care."

"You always talkin' about how you don't give a damn, couldn't give a shit and don't give a fuck. Well, let me give you a piece of advice, babygirl." Mo leaned in closer.

"You got a whole family that's barely hanging on by a thread. You are the string that holds this family together. If you don't wanna be with Victor anymore, I totally understand. Hell, I'll help you find the best lawyer in town so you can take his ass for all he got. But if there is a chance that you two can work this out, you better save your marriage, girl. Don't let this bitch come and fuck up everything you've worked so hard for. Fuck what the law say. That's yo' fuckin' husband."

Mina took in her best friend's advice but thoughts of Victor making love to Samia the way he made love to her filled her head. It was what she hated most. How could the one she loved give his love away to another? He was hers. She'd be damned if she saw another chick on his arm, but Mina was too weak and disappointed in Victor to fight. She'd given all she had. If their marriage was going to last, Victor would have to be the one to fight for their love.

Victor gripped the steering wheel of his Mercedes-Maybach. Trey Songz's *All The If's* played while he drove. He was on his way home. He'd had enough of sleeping in a hotel room alone. There was so much that still had been left unsaid between he and Mina. She didn't want to talk, and he understood her plight, but they were in the thick of love. Now was not the time to shut down and run away.

He'd fucked up. There was no denying that; but Mina needed to realize that they were past the infatuation phase. Real-life was taking place. In a marriage, unforeseen things would arise that would be out of their control. Victor never saw this coming. When he was sent the photo of Samia from an unknown email address, the wind was knocked out of his sail.

Memories of her had haunted him for years. When he'd lost her, things had happened so abruptly. He didn't even get the chance to give her a proper funeral because her body was never found. Victor never got to say goodbye or mourn her death. He had a two-year-old to take care of and a cartel to run. He couldn't show signs of weakness. He had to be strong for himself, Lelah, his family and the organization.

Yes, he had his moments where he broke down and cried. Victor begged God to take away the pain. He was young. Losing Samia nearly killed him. He could barely be around his daughter. Seeing her tiny face was a constant reminder of what he and her mother could've been, so he sent her to live with his mother.

Victor buried himself in his work. If he was going to be the leader of a drug cartel, then he was going to make sure that it was the biggest in the world. He suppressed the memory of Samia and never looked back. Then Mina came and re-entered his life. He saw her return as a sign that it was time for him to open up his heart and love again.

Victor had done a lot of dirt in his life. Some things he would never be able to shake, but Mina accepted him for who he was. She loved him despite his flaws. She quieted the demons that surrounded him. When he was with her, time stood still. Only they existed. He never wanted to leave her side. She was his one and only girl.

He never wanted to hurt her or make her cry; but when he found Samia, all of his old feelings started to rise.

She had the same bright smile and twinkle in her eye that drew him in at the age of 18 when they were arranged to be married. Her father, Luis Alavarez, was the leader of the Cali Cartel. Luis and Victor's father, Jesus, were close friends. They decided that when both their son and daughter were 18, they would combine both cartels through marriage and have the biggest drug empire in Columbia.

Unfortunately, Victor's father never got to see his son marry Samia and their families join forces. He became ill and died before the two were of age and could legally wed. Wanting to carry out his father's dying wish, Victor decided to go through with the marriage for business purposes. After his father's untimely death, the Gonzalez Cartel was vulnerable. They needed all the support they could get. He didn't want to marry some random girl he'd only met a few times, but business came before emotions.

Thankfully, by the time they said I do, Victor had fallen madly in love. He loved Samia from the moment she walked down the aisle. Beauty defined her. She was an angel on earth. The day they married was the best day of his life. Shortly after they wed, tragedy struck again and Samia's entire family was gunned down by a rival cartel called the Saldono Nation.

Samia was beside herself with grief. She had no one but Victor. With the Cali Cartel out the way, it was only a matter of time before the Saldono Nation targeted the Gonzalez Cartel. Victor thought he'd taken all the proper precautions until Samia took Lelah and snuck off to go shopping without a bodyguard. After an extensive manhunt, Victor was able to locate Lelah but was told that Samia had tried to flee and died.

17 years later, they picked up right where they left off. As soon as Victor saw her, he got amnesia quick. Shit suddenly got fuzzy and he didn't remember Mina or the vows they'd made to each other. Samia was his family. The mother of his child. How could he pretend that what they shared never existed?

Samia was comfortable and familiar. He'd tried his best not to fall into bed with her, but one-night Victor let things go too far, and he slipped up. He'd regretted it as soon as it happened. He never wanted to be the guy that cheated on his wife. But what was a man to do when he had two wives? He loved Mina and Samia. Both women were playing tug of war with his heart.

Victor pulled up to his estate and parked his car. He spotted José off in the distance playing and waved. As soon as he crossed the threshold, Mina could smell the scent of his Giorgio Armani Prive Rosē D'Arabie cologne. It enthralled her.

"Mina!" He called out her name.

Mina sat still and refused to acknowledge his presence.

"She in here!" Mo responded for her.

"Bitch." Mina quipped as he came into the kitchen.

Victor stepped into the room and filled the space with his presence. The man was larger than life. Mina wanted to hate him, but Lord, was her flesh weak. She'd never seen a man make a simple, grey, Calvin Klein logo tee, black, fitted jeans and Stan Smith Adidas look so good. His rock-hard muscles filled out the shirt. Mina tried not to look but the imprint of his dick in his jeans was calling her name.

"What's up, Mo?" Victor gave her a quick hug and kiss on the cheek.

"Hey." She stood up. "I'ma head out." She grabbed her purse. "Mina, I'll call you later, ok?"

"Mmm hmm."

Once the coast was clear, Victor sat across from Mina. An awkward silence filled the room. She wouldn't even look his way. Victor eyed her lips and breasts. Mina had a mouth like a plum. Her long hair cascaded like a waterfall past her shoulders. Victor loved her thick hair. Dark circles encompassed her eyes. Even at her worse, she was still the baddest chick in the game. She was visibly shaken by his presence. He hated the effect he had on her now.

"How are you?" He tried to spark up a conversation.

Mina ignored him and lit up another cigarette. Inhaling the smoke, she faced him and blew the smoke in his face. Victor closed his eyes and coughed. Mina was really pushing her luck. Not the one to be tried, he snatched the cigarette from her hand and put it out on the table. Mina's nostrils flared. She went to grab another cigarette but Victor picked them up before she could. Heated, he threw them on the floor and stomped them with his foot.

"I take it you don't wanna talk right now?" He shot sarcastically.

"Say what you wanna say." Mina folded her arms across her chest.

"I know you don't wanna hear none of my shit but I just really wanted to apologize."

"Victor, you can keep yo' li'l sorry-ass apology 'cause I don't accept it. You have beat my heart to death with I'm sorry."

"Well, I'm giving it to you anyway." He replied. "I'm standing here as a man tellin' you that I was wrong, that I love you and I'm still here."

"But you love her too?" Mina arched her brow.

Victor swallowed the lump in his throat. He couldn't lie to her anymore. He had to keep it 100, no matter how fucked up it was.

"I can't say that I don't." He said cautiously.

"What the fuck does that mean? It's either you do or you don't," Mina spat.

"Well, how would you feel if you were in my position?" He switched it around on her.

"This ain't about me, muthafucka. This is about you," she snapped.

"This is about me. That's why I'm sitting here talking to you now."

"Stop with the mind games. I'm not about to play with you. It's obvious you still love the bitch 'cause you haven't confirmed or denied it."

Mina's stomach contracted with humiliation. Victor had never hit her, but he was mentally abusing the fuck outta her.

"You ain't even gotta say it 'cause I already know the truth." She said after a brief pause. "So what do you think I'm supposed to do with this information? I'm just supposed to stick around and wait for you to decide which one of us you wanna be wit' like we on ElimiDATE or something?"

"Mina, I love you to death. I don't wanna lose you but I'm in a fucked up position. Honestly, I want you to rock with me through this, but I don't wanna hurt you anymore either. But I'd be lying if I said I wanted you to go do you."

"Woooooooow." Mina replied taken aback. "You something else." She chuckled in disbelief.

"See, you ask me to be honest wit' you, then you get mad when I tell you the truth. That's what pushes me away from you—"

"Uh ah," Mina waved her index finger from side to side. "Don't even try to fix yo' mouth to blame this on me! You kept all this shit a secret 'cause you knew you was on some bullshit! You was tryin' to have yo' cake and eat it too!"

"Hold up. Don't put words in my mouth 'cause nobody said that at all. Ain't nobody tryin' to blame shit on you!" Victor barked, fed up.

"You bet not," Mina scoffed, leaning back in her seat.

Victor exhaled and licked his bottom lip. He hated where they were at. He'd lost his homie, his lover and his friend. Mina gazed at him. For the first time since everything went down, she allowed herself to see the stress on his face. Victor was literally a broken man. The woman he loved more than life itself didn't love him anymore. Mina was not checking for him at all.

"Why you lookin' like that?" She let her guard down for a second.

Victor sat quiet and tried to collect himself. He wasn't an emotional type of dude but the strife between him and his wife was fuckin' him up.

"I love you, man," he confessed. "I thought what I was doing was right. I was just tryin' to protect everybody. I had tunnel vision. I didn't see it. I got so wrapped up in the shit that I lost sight of the greater good. Now I don't know what to do." He gazed deep into her hazel eyes.

"I know it's hard, and it feels like we fell out of love, but we've come too far to give up now."

"Victor... you just sat up here and told me you were in love with your dead wife." Mina looked at him like he was stupid. "What the fuck are you talkin' about?"

"I pour my heart out to you and this is how you respond?" He barked. "It's like there's no gettin' through to you. Whatever, man. Look..." Victor calmed down. "I know you ain't gon' wanna hear this, but... I invited Samia over later on this week."

"You did what?" Mina shrieked.

"She wants to scc her daughter and I think that she should."

"And you didn't think to ask me how I would feel? Oh, I forgot, my feelings don't matter. It's all about you and yo' new family," she spat.

"Stop with the dramatics. You know damn well it ain't even like that."

"I don't know shit no more when it comes to you. But I do know that bitch won't be up in here. Y'all can play husband and wife all y'all want to, but you won't be doing it up in my house."

"You do know that this is my house too?" Victor eyed her as if she were crazy.

"And?" Mina rolled her neck. "This wavy hair bitch come back and you forget all about me. Fuck my feelings, right?"

"Lelah has asked to meet her mother. I'm not going to stand in the way of that."

Mina sat quiet. She had no idea that Lelah had requested to see Samia.

"I understand you're hurt, but you gotta put your feelings aside for babygirl. This is bigger than me and you," Victor stressed.

"The fact that you just let that come out your mouth says everything to me. You don't get it." Mina rose to her feet. "And it's ok. You don't have to. Just know one day real soon you gon' look up and I'm not gon' be here." She snapped, walking away.

"You wanna see me wildin'."

-Beyoncé, "Sorry"

#12

Mina didn't want to, but after what seemed like a million calls and text messages from her mother, she was coerced out of the house. Mina did not want to deal with her mother or the public. She made that clear by not doing her makeup or combing her hair. Her hair was all over the place - just like her life - so she wore a black skull cap to cover up the mess. A pair of oversized, black Chanel shades shielded the world from seeing her red, swollen eyes. A t-shirt, leggings and Tims made up the rest of her look. Mina normally only wore stuff like this when she was running errands or lounging around the house. She was a glamour girl; but with everything going on in her life, her looks were at the bottom of her list of priorities.

Rita and Bernice insisted that she get out of the house and get some fresh air, so they all headed to Red Lobster to eat. There was no way that Mina was going to spend over an hour with her mom and aunt and not have backup. She hit Delicious up and demanded that he come too. As they were seated, Mina started to realize how much of a bad idea it was to invite him along. Delicious was no better than Rita and Bernice. The three of them together was like watching an episode of Flavor of Love.

It was the middle of the day and he thought it was appropriate to wear a reddish-brown curly wig, blue jean crop jacket, black, lace bra, low-rider jeans and heels. His whole stomach and part of his ass was out. Her mom, Rita, took the phrase Ghetto Fabulous to a whole 'nother level. Despite Mina's disapproval, she had Delicious install a head full of piss blonde, Ramen-noodle-looking, curly weave in her head. The hair was cut right at her chin and she even had the nerve to have bangs. The hair color totally washed her skin out.

Things went further downhill from there. Rita was a known label whore. If it had a logo on it, she was buying it. She had on a fake Gucci vest that she got from Frison Flea Market, which exposed the tattoo of a woman driving a sailboat on her arm. The rest of the ratchet look consisted of a pair of denim, booty shorts and matching fake Gucci boots.

Mina really sank down the rabbit hole when her Aunt Bernice hopped out of the car. It was like she was an extra from a bad Nicki Minaj video. She wore a pink, synthetic wig, bug-eyed shades, gold, lightning bolt earrings, a seafoam green crop jacket, hot pink bandeau, seafoam green, skin-tight pants with a pair of hot pink panties over them and Doc Martin boots. Mina wanted nothing more than to turn around and go home, but they'd picked her up so she was stuck. Once they were seated, Mina sank down into her seat. She prayed to God that no one would recognize that it was her with them.

"You talkin' about a bitch that's about to fuck up some biscuits!" Rita rubbed her hands together like she was Birdman.

"Garcon!" Aunt Bernice snapped her fingers, signaling the waiter.

"Oh my God," Mina groaned, wanting to disappear.

"May we have a basket of biscuits, please?" Aunt Bernice said properly.

"Sure thing, ma'am. How about we start you all off with something to drink." The waiter took out his pad and pen. "What can I get you, sir?" He focused his attention on Delicious.

"Your number and a Malibu Breeze," Delicious winked his eye.

"And you?" The waiter blushed, looking at Mina.

"I'll take a Sprite." She replied unenthusiastically.

"And you, sir?" He looked at Aunt Bernice.

"Did this nigga just call me a he?" She asked Rita.

"Uh huh, yes he did," Rita confirmed.

"Negro, this here is all woman." Aunt Bernice slid her hands down her breasts. "Don't let the smooth taste fool you."

"Forgive me. I apologize." The waiter bowed. "What can I get you, ma'am?"

"I'll have," Aunt Bernice gazed down at the drink menu. "A Bahama Mama wit' a shot of cognac."

"We don't have cognac, ma'am."

"Y'all ain't got no Yak?" She screwed up her face. "What kind of establishment is this?"

"Calm down, sister," Rita rubbed her back.

She knew how her sister could get. Aunt Bernice turned into the Incredible Hulk when she didn't have any Yak in her system.

"You can put a shot of Ciroc in there if you have it," Rita told the waiter.

"We don't." The waiter gave her a tight smile.

"Ok," Rita said, becoming annoyed. "You got some Henny, Jack, Bourbon? What you got?"

"I don't know if you're confused," The waiter looked around. "But this is Red Lobster, not Studio 54."

"Who in the hell is he talkin' to?" Rita looked at Bernice.

"Apparently, you. I guess he don't know we'll get it thumpin' up in here."

"They'll both take the Bahama Mama as it is and the basket of biscuits," Mina chimed in, about to snap.

"Thank you." The waiter picked up the drink menus. "I'll be right back."

"Oh, he for damn sure won't be gettin' no tip from me," Rita said pissed.

"Me either, wit' his bougie-ass," Aunt Bernice frowned.

"I don't know. He was kinda cute to me," Delicious smiled.

"You are not about to hit on our waiter," Mina sighed.

"Yes I am. Delicious gotta have a life too."

"I know that's right." Aunt Bernice gave him a high-five.

"I thought you were all in love with Waymon?" Mina questioned.

"Girl, Waymon ass ain't talkin' about nothin'. He still tryin' to figure out if he like dick or pussy. Ain't nobody got time for that."

"Yeah, you ain't got time to be dealin' with no confused muthafucka," Rita agreed. "Speaking of confused muthafuckas." She turned her attention to Mina. "Yo' husband still over there tryin' to make you and his dead wife sister-wives?"

"You ain't have to go there, Mama." Mina replied, pissed.

"I'm sorry, baby, but it's true. I told you not to marry no Latin lover. Them Espanolas will get you fucked up every time."

"You know I had me a Puerto Rican Papi back in the day." Aunt Bernice reminisced. "He was a fine li'l something. Pretty Ricky what they called him, but I called him El Segundo."

"Why?" Delicious asked, glued to her every word.

"'Cause, baby, that quesadilla had a long, fat—"

"Alright, that's enough," Mina held her hand up.

"Quit hatin' and let her finish," Delicious pushed her hand back down.

"Here you go." The waiter came back with their drinks and biscuits. "Are you all ready to order?"

Mina, Delicious, her mom and aunt all placed their orders and then dove into the Cheddar Bay Biscuits.

"As I was sayin' before I was rudely interrupted," Aunt Bernice grimaced at Mina. "El Segundo had a long, fat, knot. The nigga had paper! He stayed caked up. He showered me and ya mama with gifts. It didn't hurt that he also knew how to crack a woman's back. He put me in positions that I can only dream about gettin' into today."

"Well, that's a visual I'll never be able to get out of my head." Mina threw down the last of her biscuit.

"Girl, what's yo' problem?" Rita snatched up the half eaten biscuit. "You know we don't waste no Cheddar Bays 'round here." She popped the rest of it in her mouth.

"Now back to you," Aunt Bernice pointed at her niece. "What you plan on doing about li'l chimichanga and Sofia Vergara?"

"She's coming over to meet Lelah for the first time tomorrow."

"You say what now? I know damn well you ain't finna let that shit go down? I ain't raise you to be no punk," Rita hissed.

"I can't stop Lelah from seeing her mother. She's 17. She's practically grown."

"But she ain't grown yet. You aren't her biological mother but that's your goddamn daughter. You raised her. You keep on walkin' around here with this defeatist attitude and that woman gon' have yo' man, yo' house and yo' kids."

"Never that," Mina disagreed.

"Well, act like it then." Aunt Bernice spoke up. "You got some say so in this. When Victor hit you wit' that shit, you should've cussed his ass the fuck out. That bitch don't need to be in yo' house. Lelah can meet wit' her ass at a park or the zoo."

"The meeting is tomorrow. I can't back out of it now, and if I don't show up, it'll look like I'm pressed by her." Mina tried to explain. "It'll look like she won."

"Fuck it then; if you gon' let her come over, then, bitch, you better be dressed to the nines," Delicious advised. "Don't you let that bitch see you lookin' like a D battery. You betta rock all yo' jewels. Show that bitch that Victor keep you drippin' in diamonds. You betta act so unbothered by her ass that you make her uncomfortable. And even though you can't stand Victor, act like y'all are a united front. You let her catch you slippin' once, don't do it again!"

"You right." Mina nodded.

"I know I am." Delicious wrapped his arm around her as their food came.

"Here you go." The waiter placed their plates down before them. "Is there anything else I can get you?"

"Can we have another round of biscuits," Rita asked.

"Ooh," The waiter winced. "Sorry, we only give out one basket of biscuits per table now."

"You's a black ass lie!" Aunt Bernice slammed her fist down on the table. "I ain't come all the way from North County to eat just one damn biscuit! Where's the manager?"

"I am the manager."

"How you the manager and the waiter? What kind of budget billing Red Lobster is this?" Aunt Bernice asked confused.

"We were short on staff today, ma'am."

"I see you short on biscuits too!" Rita spat.

"Ma'am, I'm going to have to ask you to lower your voice. You're scaring the other diners."

"I don't give a damn about these people!" Rita shot up from her seat. "I want my damn biscuits!"

"I'm sorry, I'm gonna have to ask you to leave." The manager said politely.

"We ain't leaving until we get our goddamn biscuits!" Aunt Bernice got up too and headed over to one of the other tables. "Excuse me." She grabbed several biscuits and stuffed them into her purse. "These are our biscuits."

"Security!" The manager shouted for assistance.

"Aunt Bernice, stop!" Mina begged. "You gon' get us locked up over some damn biscuits!"

"You know I'm not related to them, right?" Delicious whispered into the manager's ear. "I got class and a fat ass."

"Uh ah! My mouth been watering all day thinkin' about these biscuits! I'ma get mine!" Aunt Bernice went from table to table grabbing biscuits while Rita ducked and dodged the security guard.

"Bernice, grab a lobster too!" Rita shouted as she made a run for the car.

"I am so sorry." Mina reached into her purse and pulled out three crisp one hundred dollar bills. "This will cover everything. Come on, Delicious! I'm gettin' the hell up outta here!" Mina picked up her plate of food and headed towards the door.

"Mina, where you going? Wait on me!" Aunt Bernice yelled, grabbing a lobster out of the tank.

We can pose for a picture, all three of us.

#13

The following day came faster than expected. Mina was a nervous wreck but she didn't let it show. As far as Victor and the kids knew, she was straight. Little did Mina know, but they all saw through her charade. Mina looked beautiful but absolutely ridiculous. She'd taken Delicious' advice and was snatched from head to toe. She looked like a 1950's movie star.

Big, voluminous curls cascaded down her back. She wore a smoky eye, Flutter lashes and a nude-pink lip. A pair of Harry Winston, 4 carat, crossover earrings and a Harry Winston diamond link bracelet shined from her wrist and ears. A stunning, $3,895, Maria Lucia Hohan "Norina", metallic, pleated, chiffon gown with a sweetheart neckline, spaghetti straps, side cutouts and a thigh-high split flowed over her silhouette. The metallic Giuseppe Zanotti, embossed, leather, three-strap, 5 inch heels highlighted her toned, caramel legs.

Victor thought she looked breathtakingly beautiful. He hadn't seen her that dolled up since their fifth year wedding anniversary party. His wife was the shit but he had no idea where she was going so dressed up. She acted like she was going to the Oscars. He wanted to tell her she was doing way too much but fear of her biting his head off kept him quiet.

He knew she was breaking out the heavy artillery to one-up Samia. He was lowkey proud of her for flossing her weight around. Victor felt bad for Samia. She had no idea what Mina had in store for her. Victor tried to keep his cool but he was nervous as well. He paced back and forth across the living room floor. Having the two women he loved come face-to-face may not have been such a good idea.

Things were guaranteed to be tense. Victor kept reminding himself that it wasn't about him and his stupid love triangle. That day was all about Lelah, but the sour expression on Mina's face made him feel like a complete ass. He shouldn't have invited Samia there. At the time, he thought it would be a cool idea, but now... not so much. Samia being in their house was only going to make matters worse between he and Mina.

Victor stood up against the wall next to her. The smell of her Bottega Veneta Parco Palladiano IV Eau de Parfum made his dick hard. Victor couldn't take his eyes off her angelic face. He was torn between Mina and Samia but Mina held the key to his heart in the palm of her hand. He prayed that they would be able to find their way back to one another, but thoughts of Samia and what they used to be filled his mind. The night they slept together was forbidden ecstasy.

She filled a void that Mina wasn't there to provide. Samia was no longer the young, inexperienced girl he married. She'd learned a few things along the way. The sex was bomb but guilt quickly set in. Flashes of Mina's face danced before his eyes as soon as he came. Victor was all over the place. He was trying to do what was best for everyone, but with each turn he made, he continued to fuck up. Victor needed to get his life under control and fast.

"My bad for all of this." He whispered into her ear.

"Too late now." Mina strolled away.

She didn't want to be near him. If he would've thought of her feelings beforehand, they wouldn't have been in this position. Once again, Victor was on his selfish shit and everyone around him was suffering the consequences.

Lelah sat anxiously by the living room window, awaiting Samia's arrival. Her palms were sweating and her stomach was in knots. Like her mother, she wore one of the prettiest outfits she owned. Lelah was serving Gossip Girl, Blair Waldorf, realness in a rose-colored, short-sleeve, cotton Gucci dress. The fresh off the runway frock had a gathered plisse bodice and ruffles along the collar, sleeves, waist, and skirt. A large flower brooch was at the neck of the dress and accented with a black ribbon. Mina was so proud of her baby girl. She was beyond courageous. Mina didn't have nearly as much strength as Lelah did at the age of 17.

"Are we having a photoshoot or are we meeting Lelah's dead mama?" José came into the formal living room eating a ham sandwich.

"Boy, shut yo' mouth," Mina warned.

"I'm just sayin'. Y'all in here lookin' like y'all on the Bold and the Beautiful."

"José… not today." Victor gave him the evil eye.

"A'ight, a'ight, I'ma chill." He plopped down on the Versace couch.

"She's here!" Lelah said excitedly.

Victor looked over at Mina. Mina inhaled deeply. *Welcome to the jungle, bitch,* she thought, situating her gown. Rosario opened the door and let Samia in. As soon as she entered, the energy in the room shifted. You could hear a pin drop; it was so quiet. Samia gazed around the massive mansion in awe. She knew Victor was doing well but she had no idea he was living so lavishly.

"Mr. Gonzalez, your guest has arrived," Rosario announced.

"Hello, everyone." Samia waved, energetically.

Everyone spoke back except Mina. She was too busy taking her in. When she caught her kissing Victor in his office, she hadn't been able to study her. There was no denying that she gorgeous. Mina could see why Victor was still sprung off the bitch. She was beautiful. That day she wore her hair back in a sleek bun. She rocked a mustard yellow, Roberto Cavalli, off-the-shoulder dress that hit mid-thigh and strappy, black, stiletto heels. Samia was an understated beauty. She didn't have to do much to grab your attention.

"How was the drive over here?" Victor asked, making small talk.

"Good," Samia replied nervously.

"Let me introduce you to everyone." Victor escorted her further inside the living room. "Samia, you remember my wife Mina."

"Yes, how could I forget?" Samia looked her up and down. "She made a very big impression the first time we met. Hello, Mina. How are you?" She extended her hand for a shake.

"Girl, you betta move yo' damn hand." Mina said at once.

Samia drew her hand back and chuckled.

Victor quickly pulled her away and introduced her to José.

"This is my son, José. He's ten."

"Hello, José. I've heard so much about you." Samia bent down and gave him a warm hug.

It was taking everything in Mina not to run and drop-kick her in the throat. She hated to see her husband's wife/mistress touch her son.

"On the strength of my mom, I would hug you longer 'cause you got a fatty but you need to fall back, ma," José remarked.

"José! What I tell you about yo' mouth, boy?" Victor grimaced.

"I'm just keepin' it real." José shrugged. "Can't a brotha keep it real?"

"Excuse my son. We accidentally dropped him on his head when he was a baby."

"It's ok," Samia laughed. "I think he's cute."

"This li'l family reunion was great, but I'm over it. Mom, can I got upstairs and play?" José begged.

"Yes, baby."

José darted up the steps and disappeared in his room.

"Last but not least, Samia this is Lelah."

Lelah rose to her feet and starred at her mother in awe. She looked just like her. They could've been twins.

"You don't remember me at all, do you?" Samia inched closer to her.

"No, ma'am." Lelah shook her head.

"You don't have to call me ma'am—"

"Oh, yes the hell she do," Mina interjected. "We raised her right up in here." She arched her brow, letting her know what was up.

"As I was sayin'," Samia cut her eyes at Mina. "Call me Samia."

"Miss Samia," Mina corrected her. "We raised Lelah to respect her elders. Ain't that right, baby?" She walked over and wrapped her arm around Victor's waist.

"Uhhhhh… yeah," he replied, confused.

Just a second before, Mina didn't want to be near him. Now she was rubbing his back like they hadn't been at each other's throats all week.

"Nice to meet you, Miss Samia." Lelah shook her hand.

"We can do better than that. Can I get a hug?" Samia's voice cracked. "I haven't seen you since you were two."

"Yes." Lelah reached over and fell into her mother's arms.

Mina watched as Lelah closed her eyes and relished the moment. She should've been happy for her but Mina was jealous. Her biggest fear was that Lelah would build a close bond with Samia and forget all about her. Mina would be beside herself with grief if that were to happen.

"You don't know how long I've waited for this moment." Samia held Lelah close.

"I never even thought this day would be possible," Lelah laughed, never wanting to let her go.

"C'mon, let's have a seat. I want to know everything about you," Samia gushed.

"Well, I'm going into my senior year of high school, then I'll be attending USC, hopefully."

"Remember, I told you she was a straight A student? Babygirl is gonna be a doctor," Victor said proudly.

"She obviously got her book smarts from me. Your father, from what I know, was terrible in school."

"Yeah, my grades were trash." Victor massaged his jaw.

"I love your dress, by the way. It's super on trend," Samia complimented her.

"Thank you. My mom bought it for me." Lelah smiled at Mina.

"Your mother has great taste," Samia replied, barely able to get the words out.

"Now, tell me some things about you. Where have you been all this time?"

Samia glanced over at Victor to see if it was ok for her to tell Lelah her story. Victor nodded his head yes. Mina caught their exchange and wanted to vomit.

"I've been hiding out in Columbia. When you were two, we were kidnapped by Ángel Ayala-Vazquez, the leader of the Saldono Nation. Ángel was responsible for the death of my entire family. They wanted to finish the job; so you and I, unfortunately, were their next target. They kidnapped us and held us captive for weeks. They beat me and threatened to kill you," Samia began to cry. "I wasn't going to let anything happen to you, so I did what I had to do."

"And what was that?" Lelah died to know.

Samia wiped her nose.

"I made one of the guards think I was going to sleep with him. So when I got him alone, I kneed him in the groin, took his gun, held him at gunpoint and then ran the hell out of there to get help. The only problem was, we were in the middle of nowhere. I was stuck in the desert with no food or water for days. I eventually passed out from dehydration and exhaustion. Some man found me, put me on the back of his truck and dropped me off at the nearest hospital. By the time I came to, your dad had rescued you and moved to the states because he thought I was dead. I had no way to get in contact with him. I didn't have a phone number or an address."

"That's messed up," Lelah said feeling bad for her. "So what have you been doing all these years?"

"Trying to survive. I had no money, no family, no nothing. That is, until your father found me. He saved me. A part of me always knew he would come back for me," Samia smiled lovingly at Victor.

Mina rolled her eyes so hard she thought they were going to pop out of her head. *Somebody kill me already,* she thought.

"I'm happy you're back and that you're alive and well." Lelah hugged Samia again.

"Me too. Now I have my daughter back." Samia squeezed her tight. "Te he echado mucho de menos mi niña Hermosa."

"I missed you too, Mom," Lelah cried.

The word mom pierced Mina's ears. *She didn't just say that,* she tried to convince herself. But Lelah had. Mina felt as if her throat had been sliced wide open.

"Look at me." Lelah dabbed her face with the back of her hand. "I'm ruining my makeup. I probably look a mess."

"You could never look a mess. You look just like me," Samia assured, wiping her face.

"Let's go upstairs so you can freshen up." Victor led Lelah up the staircase.

Samia crossed her legs and pulled out a Chanel compact mirror to check her face. Mina clocked her Prada shoes and Bottega Veneta purse.

"You sholl designer down for you to have been struggling all these years," Mina quipped, sauntering over to the bar.

She needed a stiff drink. A straight shot of cognac would do.

"You may have Victor and Lelah fooled, but I see right through you, trash box. Yo' ass is up to something. I don't know what, but I'ma find out."

"Mina-Mina-Mina." Samia snapped the compact shut. "It's bad enough you're walkin' around here like you in a Miss Teen USA pageant. Please don't come for me unless I send for you," she warned.

"Send for these nuts, bitch. You in my house."

"Not for long," Samia chuckled. "Can I tell you a secret?" She made her way over to where Mina was standing.

"What? That you're a lesbian. I already knew that."

"I'm gonna get my family back," Samia leaned forward and whispered like a serial killer. "Your days are numbered around here, sweetheart."

"Bitch, you betta back up off me. I will punch you in the pussy," Mina advised. "Victor ain't checkin' for you."

"Is that right?" Samia chuckled.

"Did I stutter? You heard exactly what I said. Don't make me call immigration on yo' thirsty-ass," Mina giggled. "As a matter-of-fact, why don't you run yo' butt back across the border and play in traffic? Fresh-off-the-boat-ass bitch."

"Oh, you think that's funny? Did you laugh when you found out I had Victor in my bed not once but twice?" Samia smiled like a Cheshire cat.

"Girl, bye. You lying. Victor said it only happened once."

Samia hung her head low and cracked up laughing.

"And you really believe that? You're dumber than I thought."

The way she spoke let Mina know she was telling the truth. Victor had lied to her again. Mina was devastated. For the first time since she said I do, she regretted marrying him, but she wasn't going to let Samia know she'd won this round.

"Bitch, fuck you and yo' Rest In Peace-ass pussy," Mina shot. "I don't give a damn if Victor fucked you 10 times. You're an easy lay, bitch. Anybody can have you. Victor is my husband. Look where he's at. He's here with me. So you can miss me with that foolishness. You're a non-muthafuckin' factor, bitch."

"You have no idea who you're dealing with, do you?" Samia cocked her head to the side. "I'm in the major leagues, sweetheart, and you haven't even made it to home base. So let me give you a piece of advice. Save yourself the embarrassment and bow out gracefully."

Just when Mina was about to throw her drink in Samia's face, Lelah walked back in.

"You lucky, bitch." Mina hissed underneath her breath.

"Y'all good? Y'all ain't fighting, are you?" Lelah looked back and forth between the two of them.

"No, of course not. Mina and I were just coming to an understanding. Isn't that right, Mina?" Samia winked her eye.

"Where's your father?" Mina ignored Samia's snide remark.

"Right here." Victor smiled, happy that she and Samia didn't kill each other while he was gone.

"Mom, can you do me a favor?" Lelah asked.

"Yes." Mina and Samia answered in unison.

Mina scowled. If there was a knife next to her, she would've stabbed Samia in the neck.

"I was talkin' to Mina," Lelah giggled uncomfortably.

"Yes, baby," Mina placed her drink down.

"Can you take a picture of us?" She handed her cellphone to Mina.

"Sure, love." Mina placed the phone up to her face so she could get the perfect visual of Lelah and her father.

"Samia, get in the picture." Lelah gestured for her to come over.

Mina's hand dropped down to her side. What had she done in her previous life to deserve such disrespect from the people she loved? Did Lelah not get that seeing her, Samia and Victor together with her on the outs foreshadowed her future? What did she have to do, wear her teeth as confetti, peel her skin off and make it her own? She'd do it if it meant she'd be able to keep her family. Mina couldn't help feeling like she'd been here before. This was all too familiar.

Samia sashayed over and stood opposite of Lelah and grinned. Her plan was working. It was just a matter of time before Mina was out the picture for good.

"Me and my baby we gon' be alright."

-Beyoncé, "Sorry"

#14

After Samia left, Mina didn't utter a word to Victor. She walked around as if he wasn't even there. He figured she was just in her feelings about the meeting. Victor sympathized with her emotions. It had to have been tough to see Lelah call another woman mom. His heart broke for her when he heard her say it. Mina had stepped up to the plate and raised her as if she'd birthed her herself. She must've felt like her entire world was coming to an end.

Having Mina give him the silent treatment was the worst feeling ever. He truly missed having his best friend by his side to talk to. Whenever he had a problem, she was the first person he consulted. He didn't trust anyone else with his thoughts or feelings. He needed her to help him through this, but how could he ask the woman he was hurting for help? He couldn't. Victor had to figure this whole thing out himself.

He tried weighing the pros and cons of being married to each woman. The problem was: neither woman outweighed the other. They both were perfect in his eyes. Samia was the first woman he'd ever given his heart too and Mina was the one who brought him back to life. The biggest difference between them was that Victor knew he could live without Samia. He'd proven that to be true. The mere thought of living a day without Mina was the equivalent of dying a slow death.

He couldn't do it. He longed to sleep next to her. Not being able to touch her was driving him insane. There was no him without her. She was his reason for living. Victor wished he could turn back the hands of time. He would've loved Mina so much better. He would've let go of his past for her.

The damage was done. He'd fucked up and fumbled her heart. Thank God there was still time to mend the broken pieces of her heart. He had to let her know that with her was where he needed and wanted to be. Yeah, he still had love for Samia, but he was in love with Mina. There was a major difference. Mina was the woman he wanted to grow gray and old with. Victor jumped out of his sleep.

He'd been tossing and turning all night. Mina was on his mind heavy. He had to talk to her. They had to talk this thing out. He couldn't go another day with them being apart. He wanted his wife. He'd been foolish to think that he could replace her with another woman.

Victor didn't care what it took, he would fight tooth and nail to get Mina back. Anxious, he walked down the hallway to their bedroom. His boxer/briefs cupped his firm ass and thick, fat, juicy dick. Victor lightly tapped on the door. When he didn't get a response, he quietly cracked open the door.

"Mina… you awake?" He crept over to the bed and pulled the covers back.

To his surprise, it was empty. Curious as to where she was at, he went down to the kitchen. Mina was known to snack in the middle of the night when she was upset. Victor checked the kitchen, movie room, her in-home salon but Mina was nowhere to be found. Victor could hear his heart beat out his chest. She'd warned him that one day he'd look up and she'd be gone.

Like most men, he never thought she would go through with it. Victor raced back up to their bedroom and checked her closet. Half of her clothes were gone. He became dizzy with worry. Now he knew exactly how Mina felt the night she couldn't find him. Victor rushed to the kids' room. Lelah was sound asleep but José was gone. He didn't know what the hell was going on. Victor located his phone and called Mina. His call went straight to voicemail.

"Fuck!" He threw his phone against the wall.

His iPhone shattered and broke into a hundred pieces on the floor. Victor held his head in agony. Mina was killing him. He felt like he was having a heart attack. This was the worst pain he'd ever felt. He knew damn well Mina didn't leave and take their son with her. That was the ultimate no-no. She swore if anything ever happened between them that she would never involve the kids. He'd gone back on his word when he promised never to lie or cheat, so it was only fair she went back on hers.

That didn't stop him from being enraged. Victor dragged himself into his master bathroom. He was so mad that a single tear slipped from his eye. A look of shock was etched on his face when he entered the bathroom. Mina had left him a note. Written on the mirror in pink lipstick was:

You fucked her twice, huh? Did you not think I would find out the truth? I gave you everything and all you did was lie in return. It's ok, me and my baby gon' be alright. You can have Samia, this house and this life. I'm done.

Victor slid down to the floor. He knew the way he was living was wack, but how could Mina just pick up and leave him sick like that? She had to know that what she was doing would kill him. Victor only had himself to blame. His fuckboy behavior had landed him in his 63-million-dollar mansion alone. He'd jeopardized everything he loved - and lost.

The six months in Columbia locating Samia, all the lies, cheating, playing with Mina's heart, none of it was worth it. It was a shame that it took him losing her for him to realize what he'd done was wrong. Lying to Mina wasn't worth the anger and hurt he felt.

Victor had mixed emotions. On one hand, he hated her for leaving and taking their son. He didn't know where they were at and if or when they were coming back. It wasn't like Victor could go to the police for help. Mina was playing dirty. He didn't even know she had it in her to be so spiteful.

The other part of him understood why she dipped. He'd done things that he was ashamed of, like sleeping with Samia more than once. Victor knew if he told Mina the truth, she'd never forgive him. With his knees up to his chest, Victor cried like a baby. He was torn up. He'd lost his best friend and his soulmate. Empty walls couldn't hold their house together. He needed Mina to come home. They were meant to last forever but she was gone. Now the only thing he could do was live with the fact that she was gone and he'd done her wrong forever.

"He only want me when I'm not there. He better call Becky with the good hair."

-Beyoncé, "Sorry"

#15

At first Mina thought escaping to her parents' house was the most logical thing to do, but two weeks into her staying there, she quickly regretted her decision. She needed peace and quiet. There was no way in hell she was getting that while living with Rita and Ed. They were loud from the moment they woke up till the moment they went to bed. Nightfall was the worst. For her parents to be in their 60's, they still got it poppin' every night.

They were loud and nasty with it too. Closing the door or putting the pillow over her head didn't deafen the sounds of her mother moaning and groaning. All night long she'd hear nothing but *"oooooooh, Ed, get it daddy, work the middle, how many licks does it take to get to the center?"* Mina wanted to gouge her ears out. She hated it there; but being at home with Victor and Lelah wasn't an option either.

Mina couldn't bear to look at either of their faces. They'd both cut her deep. Because of them, she lie unable to move. She'd spent the last two weeks in bed - only getting up to bathe and eat enough food to survive. If it hadn't been for her son, she literally would've ended it all. There was nothing else to live for. Her insides had been gutted out and fed to vultures.

Since they didn't give a fuck about her feelings, Mina decided to be selfish and not give a fuck about theirs. Victor could take care of Lelah himself. He could be the one to cater to her every need. Mina was done being mother of the year. For 10 years she'd taken care of everyone else. She'd put them all before herself. Well, no more. Samia was back from the dead. They both seemed to love her so much. She could pick up where Mina left off. It seemed like that was what they wanted anyway.

After 10 years of being together, it fucked Mina up that Victor could be torn between her and another woman. She'd held him down through thick and thin, then Samia's old Port of Miami lookin' ass returns and all of that is thrown out the window. Even though he was mixed, Mina was so tired of black men choosing light over right. What had Samia done besides show up and be pretty for him to be so confused?

Mina was the one who stuck by his side and went through the trenches with him. Samia wasn't the one who took care of home, raised both of his children while running several businesses and still managed to suck his dick every night. All she did was show up with a sob story, bat her long lashes, flaunt her big, fake boobs, flip her silky, straight hair and smile. Mina didn't know what it was about women of other ethnicities that drove black men so crazy.

It was almost like they were glamourized by the lightness of their skin. She was over being any man's second choice. Mina Elise Matthews was nobody's option. She was the main course. That's why she ran away. She had to teach Victor a lesson. He couldn't go around treating her like shit and think he was going to get away with it. If he could so easily disregard her, their marriage and everything they stood for, then she'd do the same.

She hated to involve their son into their drama, but taking José was the one sure way she knew she could hurt him. Her plan worked. Victor was incensed with anger. He didn't play when it came to his children. Mina taking José and not answering his calls was her way of declaring war. Mina had even gone so far as to tell him if he tried to come get him she'd call the police on his ass.

Victor wanted to kill her and he'd made it clear that her ass was grass when he saw her. She had life, her edges,

Jesus and him fucked up if she thought what she was doing was cool. He wanted to be back with her, but after this stunt, he wasn't so sure. He no longer knew who Mina was. Victor eventually found out where they were because José called him to let him know they were ok.

When they first got to his grandparents' house, José was cool with staying there. He didn't want his mother to feel like he'd abandoned her too. She needed someone there to comfort her. But after two weeks, José had enough. He missed his room, his video games and his friends. It was summer vacation and there he was held up in the house with his ratchet-ass grandparents, sickly great-grandmother and depressed mother. José was tired of smelling like Bengay and mothballs. No slight to his mother, but he wanted to go home!

Like any other day since they'd been there, José found his mom laying on his grandmother's plastic-covered couch, swaddled in a cover. Mina's face was pressed against the plastic. Every time she exhaled, her breath left a fog imprint. José sat beside his mother and stared at her. She was watching old episodes of Half & Half. She lay there as stiff as a board. She almost looked comatose.

"Mom," he said softly.

"Huh?" Mina replied barely audible.

"When are we going home?"

"José, go sit down." Mina said, not in the mood for a bunch of questions.

All she wanted was to be left alone so she could sulk in peace.

"Can I call Pop so he can come get me?" José asked on edge.

"No."

"But why not? I don't wanna be here no more. I wanna go home. I wanna see my dad."

"Didn't I tell yo' ass no?!" Mina shot up furious. "We're not going home! So stop asking me that!"

"Mina, why are you yellin' at that boy?" Rita yelled from the kitchen.

She was preparing lunch.

"Mind your business, Mama. Ain't nobody talkin' to you. José, go sit down," Mina commanded.

"No." He responded with a sudden fierceness.

"What did you say to me?" Mina screwed up her face.

"I said no. I'm callin' my dad." José went to go grab the house phone.

"Didn't I tell yo' li'l grown-ass to go sit down?" Mina jumped up from the couch and snatched him by the arm.

"Mom, stop! Let me go!" José cried trying to break away. "I wanna go home! I wanna see my dad!"

"What the hell are you doing?" Rita walked up on Mina.

"This ain't got nothing to do with you, Mama!" Mina seethed, turning her attention back to José.

Her grip was so tight on his arm that it started to turn red.

"You ain't never going home! Your father doesn't love us anymore! It's just me and you now!" She sobbed.

Mina knew she was trippin' but she couldn't stop herself. She had officially lost her mind.

"Why would you tell him that? Baby, that's not true." Rita tried to comfort José. "Your father loves you very much."

"No, he doesn't, 'cause if he did, he wouldn't have lied to us! He wouldn't have cheated on me! Your father broke our family apart; so stop asking me can you go home! It's not happening! We don't have a home anymore!"

"You don't have a home anymore! My dad still loves me!" José shot, spitefully. "It ain't my fault he don't wanna be with you no more! Look at the way you actin'! If I was him, I wouldn't want to be with you either—"

Heated that he'd have the audacity to speak to her that way, Mina popped José in the mouth several times. She normally didn't hit him, but that day he deserved it.

"Talk to me like that again and see what happen," she warned.

"I don't care what you say! I'm callin' my dad!" José cried like a baby.

His defiance enraged Mina.

"Fine!" She shoved his arm away. "You wanna go with your trifling-ass daddy, then go ahead! I don't care! Do what you wanna do." Mina threw her hands up in the air.

"José, baby, go ahead; call your dad and get yo' stuff together. I need to talk to ya mama," Rita instructed.

"Yes, ma'am." José wept as his little chest heaved up and down.

Once he disappeared down the hall, Rita turned to her daughter and said, "You done lost yo' mind, girl."

"Gone, Mama. I ain't got time for no lecture today." Mina said feeling like she was having an outer body experience.

"You can't keep that boy away from his father. I don't care what y'all going through. It ain't right! Now I don't mind you staying here, but you ain't gon' be pullin' no shit like that in my house!"

"You act like you ain't never been through shit. You act like you ain't never walked a day in my shoes. Yo' life ain't picture-perfect." Mina looked her up and down with disgust.

"Mina, you ain't the first woman to get cheated on and you won't be the last. All men cheat, so put your big girl panties on and deal with it."

Mina couldn't believe the words that were coming out of her mother's mouth. She needed sympathy and support, but instead, all her mother had to give was a sermon on accepting a man's shitty behavior.

"Whose side are you on? I thought I was your daughter. Shouldn't my feelings come first?"

"Not over my grandbaby's," Rita clarified. "His feelings gon' always come first. What you just did was wrong, dead-ass wrong. I didn't raise you like that."

"Oh, I get it," Mina smirked. "I forgot, this type of shit is ok with you. You the person that let daddy kiss me with the same lips he used to kiss Ann's pussy with." Mina referred to her half-sister, Meesa's, deceased mother.

Feeling like she'd been verbally bitch-slapped by her daughter, Rita gasped. Before Mina realized what happened, her mother slapped her so hard she whipped around, doing a triple axel and fell to the ground.

"And my fist gon' be the same fist that send yo' ass to the grave if you ever speak to me like that again," Rita warned, trembling with anger.

"What the hell is going on in here?" Ed walked in bewildered. "I can hear y'all all the way from the driveway."

"Your daughter about to meet her maker! She keep on fuckin' wit me!" Rita stormed out of the room.

"I'm not too perfect to ever feel this worthless."

-Beyoncé, "Hold Up"

#16

Hot tears ran down Mina's cheeks as she held a pack of frozen peas to her face. The slap her mother had given her was so forceful it caused the left side of her face to swell up. Mina couldn't believe her mother had hit her. She knew she deserved it, but it didn't stop her face or her heart from being bruised. All she wanted was for someone to see her and recognize her pain. Her mother knew all too well what it felt like to be cheated on. Her father had a whole baby on her with his mistress.

It was years later that he found out he had a daughter; but that pain of knowing that some other woman had a piece of her man had to have hurt Rita. She should've sympathized with her daughter's agony. Instead, she scolded her as if she were a child. Mina refused to see that she was behaving like one.

Rita had to defend her grandchild. Mina had gone off the deep end. She'd never behaved like an abusive mother towards her child before. It felt like she was losing her family members - one person at a time. Mina wanted to go and apologize to José for the way she'd acted but now wasn't the time. The wound was still too fresh.

She'd make it up to her son eventually. Mina was just too embarrassed by her behavior to face him. She couldn't bear to see the look of disdain in his eyes. Mina needed help. She needed a shoulder to lean on. *Lord, help me,* she begged. *I don't wanna lose my sanity.* God, must've heard her prayers because her phone started to ring. Mina looked down at the screen with her good eye. Meesa was FaceTiming her.

"Hello?" She placed the phone up to her face.

"Damnnnnnnnn... you got knocked the fuck out!" Meesa exclaimed, dying laughing.

"Ha-ha-ha, funny," Mina rolled her eyes.

"I'm sorry," Meesa stopped laughing. "I had to get that one out. I couldn't help it. But nah, for real, girl. How yo' eye feel?" She quoted a line from the movie Baby Boy.

"It's alright. It's alllllllllright," Mina played along with her sister.

"Chile, Daddy called and told me what happened."

"His big-mouth-ass can't keep shit to himself," Mina grimaced.

"I can't believe you said that to Rita and still alive to talk about it," Meesa said surprised. "I would've never stepped to yo' mama like that. You seen how big yo' mama arms is? One arm is like the size of John Cena's."

"Trust me, I learned my lesson."

"What's going on, honey bunches of oats? You need me to come down there and chin check that nigga? 'Cause you know I'll do it. I'll dropkick the shit out that muthafucka."

Mina bugged up laughing. Talking to her sister was exactly what she needed. She missed Meesa. It had been ages since they saw one another. Despite the distance between them, they made it their business to talk no less than once a week. Mina loved her sister dearly. They were the mirror image of one another.

"Nah, it's cool. I can handle Victor on my own."

"You sure, 'cause umm," Meesa popped her lips. "It looks to me like you fighting a losing battle."

"Meesa, I don't know what's wrong with me." Mina broke down. "Everything is so fucked up. My husband isn't even my husband anymore. We're not even technically married. My daughter is callin' another bitch mama. And yeah, she's technically her mother, but I don't give a fuck. That's my daughter. José hates me and it's all my fault. Plus, this bitch ain't really who she seem to be. It's just too much. I don't know what I'ma do."

"The first thing you're gonna do is calm down," Meesa cautioned. "I know it's hard but you can't let your circumstances beat you. This ain't nothin' but the devil trying to wreak havoc on your life. That sneaky muthafucka has come to kill and destroy. You gotta rebuke him in the name of Blue Ivy, girl. You can't let him win, girl. You gotta be strong. And I know that's easier said than done. Especially, when your heart feels like it's being stomped on by a Gabourey Sidibe. Being cheated on by the man you love and adore ain't no joke. Trust me, I know. I get it. But you can make it through this. You're a tough girl. Remember, Daddy ain't raise no punks."

Mina cracked a smile and laughed.

"Oww... don't make me laugh. It hurts." She situated the pack of frozen peas on her face.

"You didn't ask, but my advice to you is to let José go back home since that's where he wants to be. It doesn't mean he doesn't love you anymore. He just misses his father. Let him go home and you take this time to get yourself together. Let everything that's happened digest in your system and figure out what it is you want to do. Besides, you don't want your baby seeing you like this."

"I don't," Mina sniffed.

"And apologize to your mother before she DDT yo' ass again," Meesa placed her hand over her mouth and snickered.

"Fuck you." Mina hit her with the middle finger.

"I love you, sis, and you know I'm here whenever you need me," Meesa said sincerely.

"I know. I love you too."

An hour later, Mina stood in the doorway and watched as Victor's car pulled into the driveway. She didn't want José to go, but like her sister said, it was the right thing to do. José picked his duffle bag off the floor and placed it onto his shoulder. He hadn't uttered a word to his mother since the incident. He wanted to be as far away from her as possible. Mina saw the apprehension on his face as he neared her. At that moment, she felt like the shittiest mother on the planet.

"You got all your stuff?" She asked somberly.

"Yeah." José avoided eye contact with her.

"You got your toothbrush and your—"

"I said, yeah," José snapped. "Can I go now?"

Mina choked back the tears in her throat. She'd really messed up this time.

"José, I'm sorry. Mommy didn't mean what she said." She tried to reach out and stroke his curly hair.

José reared his head back so she couldn't touch him.

"Pop's waiting for me. I gotta go." He dashed past her and opened the screen door.

Victor stood outside the car gazing up at the house. For a brief second, he and Mina caught eyes. Victor quickly looked away. For the first time since they met, he couldn't stand the sight of her face. José had told him what she'd said. Victor couldn't fathom that she'd let such vile words slip through her lips. She knew how much he loved his kids.

Mina was hurting and she had every right to be angry, but trying to turn their son against him was unforgiveable. Victor would never be able to look at her the same way again.

Emptiness:

As a human condition, is a sense of generalized boredom, social alienation and apathy.

"She works for the money."

-Beyoncé, "6 Inch"

#17

A full month passed before Mina returned to the shop. Taking Meesa's advice, she'd taken the time to gather her emotions and figure out what it was she wanted to do. She'd gone over her decision time and time again in her head. There was only one solution to her problem. Now that she'd made her choice, it was time to get back to work. Mina was not about to let no nigga come before her grind or stop her coin. She had to take care of herself.

And yes, she often found herself wanting to reach out to Victor just so she could hear the sound of his deep, raspy voice. This was the most time they'd spent apart since they linked back up. Not being able to speak to him or have him hold her in his arms was a cross she never wanted to bear. Just a minute ago he was her baby, now she didn't even know him at all. He'd morphed from her lover, her champion, her king to her torturer, enemy and opponent.

She and Victor were stuck in a limbo of emptiness and hate. Mina tried to pray her anger and resentment away but it wouldn't budge. Victor had really done a number on her. There was no way that they could come back from his betrayal. From the looks of it, he was done with her too. She hadn't heard from him or seen him since he came to pick José up that fateful day. It was funny to her how he had the nerve to have an attitude with her. He acted like she was the one who lied and broke his heart. Niggas were funny that way. In Mina's eyes, his ass needed to grow up and take responsibility for his actions. He'd done his dirt. Now it was time for him to lie in it.

Thank God Lelah and José were old enough to communicate with her on their own. Things were still pretty tense between her and the kids. They felt like she'd abandoned them, which she had. Mina tried to make them understand that with the mental state she was in, being around them was no good. She could barely take care of herself, let alone them too. They might've been upset, but for once in her life, Mina had to be selfish for her own, personal sake. They didn't need to see her pulling out her hair and fussing and fighting with Victor. When she returned home, she'd be a better person for the time she spent away.

Mina hadn't just abandoned her kids. She'd abandoned her shop and her employees. Thankfully, they were grown and mature enough to understand what she was going through. Delicious stepped up and took over the shop in her absence. Mina thanked God for him. He'd been a godsend throughout the whole ordeal. Mina didn't know what she'd do without him.

Fully ready to get back into the swing of things, Mina stepped inside the salon feeling like a bag of money. For weeks, she lived in pajamas and sweats. It felt good to comb her hair and put on some decent clothes. Dressed in all black like an omen, she stomped her way into the shop like she was Naomi Campbell on the runway. Mina didn't even get one foot through the door when she had to stop and do a double take.

Nah, I got the wrong place, she thought. Flummoxed, she stepped back outside and checked the name on the building. Sure enough, she was at Mina's Joint Salon and Spa. Mina took off her Dior, two-tone, metallic, aviator shades and pulled the front door open once more. Her mouth almost dropped to the floor.

Before her eyes, during the middle of the day, was her entire staff partying like it was 1999. Big Freedia's *Explode* was playing so loud, Mina could barely think straight. A brand-new, frozen margarita machine was on the receptionist desk as soon as you walked in. Streamers and balloons were everywhere. Her one-of-a-kind chandelier had been replaced with a plastic disco ball. Delicious had one of those strobe lights you can buy from Party City plugged into the wall.

They were all partying so hard that they didn't even notice that she had come in. All of her employees, except Jodie, were on the makeshift dance floor making their asses clap. Jodie sat off to the side in a knee-length dress with her face planted inside her Bible. Mina wasn't at all surprised to find Delicious and Janiya in the center of the all the madness. Their ratchet-asses were bent over, twerking for two oily, buff men dressed in hot pink, satin thongs and dog collars. Mina wondered if they had been having day parties the whole time she was gone. If so, Delicious was dead. Mina flicked on the switch.

"Who turned on the lights?" Delicious stood up and shielded his eyes from the glare.

"I did! You Smurf lookin' muthafucka!" Mina snatched the cord to the sound system out the wall.

Delicious had dyed his blonde hair aqua blue.

"Uh oh! Time to go!" Delicious tried to run out the backdoor.

"Bring dat ass here, boy!" Mina grabbed him by the collar of his lace shirt. "You ain't going nowhere. Tell the pit crew it's time to go."

"Tyra mail! This is not a test!" Delicious grabbed his megaphone. "Mutha Hen is in the building! I repeat, the Louboutin Lass, Prada Playa is here! If you're not an employee or a client, I'm sorry, but this is where we bid you adieu!"

"Awww… we gotta go too?" One of the male, exotic strippers whined. "We was just about to do the Bend and Snap."

"You ain't gotta go but you gotta get the hell outta here!" Mina demanded. "Unless you want me to use this on you." She pulled a pink TASER from out of her purse.

The dancers grabbed their feather boas, tip money and ran out the door. Once everything was settled, Mina sat her staff down. They all looked like scared children about to get a whoppin'. Slowly, Mina walked back and forth down the aisle with the TASER in her hand. She didn't utter one word as she stared them all down. She wanted to instill the fear of God in them.

"I leave for a month to handle some personal business and this is what I come back to, my employees having a freak fest in the middle of my salon? Delicious, I trusted you and this is what you do to me?"

"Mina, I swear. It's not as bad as it looks—"

"Shut the hell up, gay Sisqo!" Mina sparked the TASER near his face.

"No-no-no-no-no-no, please, not the face," he winced. "It's my money maker."

"But ain't Sisqo gay?" Neosha furrowed her brows.

"You shut up, Keyshia Cole." Mina pointed the TASER at her. "I got a cool drink for you." She eyed a bottle of bleach.

"You know this is against the law?" Janiya asked.

"Say something else! Say something else, li'l nigga!" Mina stomped her foot and imitated Pinky from the movie Next Friday.

The staff bucked their eyes and looked at her like she was insane. Mina calmed down and ran her fingers through her hair.

"I get it. Everybody likes to party. Everybody likes to have a good time, but when did my shop turn from a high-end salon to a gay Carnival cruise?"

"Umm, Mina," Jodie cleared her throat and raised her hand. "May I object here? I would like to point out that I did not participate in this debauchery. I told them it was a bad idea. You know, Luke Chapter 1 verse 5 says." Jodie thumbed through her Bible.

"It's ok, Jodie, I get it." Mina stopped her.

She was not in the mood for Jodie to be quoting Bible verses.

"I should fire all y'all and hire a whole new staff."

"Now I wouldn't say all that," Delicious rebutted.

"Mina, please don't fire us," Janiya cried. "I need this job. My baby need some new shoes."

"You ain't even got no baby!" Mina snapped, ready to punch her in the titty.

"Well, if I had one she'd need some," Janiya continued to cry.

"Oh stop it. Your tiny eyes can't even produce tears," Mina frowned. "Y'all think I'm mad?" She looked around at each of their faces.

"Yeah." They all nodded, solemnly.

"Well, I'm not. I'm cool. I'm straight. All I wanna know is..." Mina paused for dramatic effect. "Why the hell wasn't I invited? A bitch wanna party too!" She cracked up laughing.

Everyone slumped in their seats with a sigh of relief.

"Ooooh, bitch!" Delicious wiped the sweat from his brow. "I'm happier than a Make a Wish kid at Disney Land. You had me going there for a second, girl. I thought I was about to be on the unemployment line."

"You know I could never fire you. I used to be fat and you're gay, we're supposed to be friends. Nigga, we stuck together like glue." Mina squeezed him tight. "Somebody fix me a margarita. A bitch need a drink."

Janiya didn't hesitate to fix her one. Mina let the frosty drink slide down her throat with ease.

"Mmm... that's good. We should'a been had one of these."

"I told you she was gon' like it!" Delicious patted himself on the back.

"I'm just glad you back, Mina. We missed you." Neosha hugged her. "We've been worried sick about you."

"I can't tell," Mina scoffed. "I'm happy to be back, though. I couldn't spend one more day cooped up in that house with Rita and Ed. Chile, they are driving me crazy."

"You still don't have any plans on going home?"

"Nope." Mina smacked her lips.

"Well, since you ain't going home no time soon, you should go out with us tonight," Neosha suggested.

"That's what's up. I need something fun to do."

"Uh ah," Delicious turned up his face. "You know damn well she can't go."

"Oh fuck, I forgot." Neosha slapped her hand against her forehead.

"What?" Mina eyed them both, confused.

"We going to 1108 tonight, girl. It's hip hop night."

"So." Mina curled her upper lip. "I don't care shit about going to Victor's club. That nigga ain't stopping nothin' over here. As a matter-of-fact, it's a good thing y'all are going there. Victor and I have some unfinished business we need to take care of anyway."

"Jesus, be a fence," Delicious prayed. "What the hell are you about to do?"

"You'll see. You will see."

"Six inch heels. She walked in the club like nobody's business."

-Beyoncé, "6 Inch"

#18

Mina Elise Gonzalez was a brand new woman.
She'd gone through a complete transformation in a matter
of hours. It was out with the old and in with the new. She'd
shed her old skin and hair and was birthed a new woman.
She didn't want any memory of her former self. The old
Mina was dead and gone. She'd died the moment she found
out her husband was a fake. Mina was on her new shit. She
and Delicious, along with Janiya and Neosha, stepped into
1108 like the major key alert they were.

Mina was feeling herself to the fullest. Delicious
had cut and styled the fuck out of her hair. After much
debate, he hesitantly chopped all 18 inches of it off. Mina
now rocked a short, brown, layered, pixie haircut. Wispy
bangs framed her heart-shaped face. Since they were hitting
up her estranged husband's club, Mina had to be extra.
Cutting off her hair wasn't enough. She had to hit Victor
where it hurt.

She was always fresh to death, but Mina kept it
classy at all times. She never showed too much skin. That
night, things would be different. Mina was going to show

her ass, literally. A pair of $520 Thierry Lasry butterfly sunglasses covered her hazel eyes. On her lips was a berry-colored matte lipstick. The black, fitted, Balenciaga leather jacket, white cami, stonewashed Alexander McQueen booty shorts and $1,075 Gianvito Rossi, patent leather, 6-inch, ankle boots gave her the much needed sex appeal she desired.

The shorts were so short they barely covered her ass cheeks. The bottom of her firm ass peeked out from under the denim fray of the shorts. Her long, lean legs were on full display for everyone to see. Victor was sure to shit a brick when he saw her. He never liked for her to show too much skin. Mina couldn't wait to see the look on his face. He'd never see her coming.

Mina strutted inside the club with her Edie Parker, Lara Confetti acrylic backlit clutch bag inside her stiletto manicured hand. The dark club was lit by red lights. Mina looked around to see if she could spot Victor anywhere. He was nowhere to be found. She did spot Julisa though. She was sure that she would notify her boss that his wife was in the building.

Mina and the crew made their way to the center of the dance floor. She was a dangerous muthafucka with a pocket full of money and Henny in her system. There was no telling what she might do. 1108 was poppin'. There were so many people it was hard to breathe. The energy was amazing. Mina was hype as hell. Her and her crew were the epitome of squad goals. All eyes were on them. Mina moved her arms like she was running in place as Plies' *Ran Off On Da Plug Twice* bumped. The song was her shit.

"I'm just vibin' in the Ritz Carlton! Got the stick, call the Ritz Carlton! Count a mil ridin' Ritz Carlton! Wanna fuck me, baby, pull up at the Ritz Carlton!" She sang at the top of her lungs.

Mina danced as if she were in a music video. Everyone was watching her, but for Mina, nothing else existed except her and the music. She could dance her ass off. Delicious, Neosha and Janiya could barely keep up with her. Each sway of her hips matched the bass drum of the beat. Lightning struck every time she moved. She felt young and vibrant.

Mad dudes kept trying to buy her drinks and get her number but Mina couldn't be bothered. She was there to enjoy the music and stunt on her husband. She was having a ball until she noticed Samia staring at her out of the corner of her eye. The only thing that Mina hated more than drugstore makeup was that bitch. Samia being the messy bitch she was, smiled and waved while finishing up a text.

Mina stopped dancing and lowered her shades to the tip of her nose. *What the fuck is she doing here,* she thought. Then Mina noticed she had a headset on and a clipboard in her hand. *This bitch work here,* she fumed. Victor had once again failed to tell her this bit of important information. They hadn't been on speaking terms, but this was still something she needed to know.

Samia had infiltrated their entire life. Mina hated her beautiful-ass. The bitch was everywhere. Mina couldn't shake her. She wasn't playing when she said she was going to get her family back. The chick was on a mission. She was most certainly putting in more of an effort to be with Victor than Mina was. As far as Mina was concerned, she could have his sorry-ass. The man she married vanished the moment he walked out the door and left her for six months.

They'd never be the way they were. Victor and Mina were done. Seeing Samia there at the club was the nail in the coffin. He could now lower her casket into the ground and cover her body in dirt.

Little did Mina know, but Victor had been watching her from the security monitor the entire time. He was thoroughly confused as to why she was there. It was obvious she was trying to prove some point. She'd cut off all her hair and was dressed like a prostitot. Victor was over her and her erratic behavior. If she was trying to kill him, she'd succeeded. She could be upset, but he was over her trying to punish him for his sins.

Victor left his office and made his way through the crowded club. Mina could feel his commanding presence as he neared. Wealth and dominance exuded from his pores. Mina tried to pretend like he didn't have a hold on her anymore. That theory was proven wrong the closer he came. She couldn't steady her breathing. She was excited to see him. She couldn't fight it.

No man could rock a two-piece, black and gray Tom Ford suit like him. The suit was tailored to perfection. His low cut and perfectly-trimmed beard gave Mina chills. The Audemars Piguet watch she'd bought him for Valentine's Day the previous year rested comfortably on his wrist. Mina couldn't take her eyes off the bulge inside his pants. His dick was cocked to the right and resting on his thigh. The thought of her using her mouth to take his pants off made Mina's panties moist.

Visions of how she used to ride his dick like a solider filled her head. He used to love when she was on top. The visual of her rotating her hips as he came deep inside used to send him to new heights of ecstasy. She'd fuck it and suck it for hours without ever having enough. Victor's cock was magically delicious. She missed the way he used to have his way with her.

Victor could front all he wanted. Even though he tried to play it off, he thought about Mina every day. Just seeing shawty live in the flesh had him fantasizing about all the things he wanted to do. His dick grew 10 extra inches as soon as he laid eyes on her face. Mina had him feenin' for her love. It didn't take a rocket scientist to see that he still had feelings for her. Every time his phone rang, he prayed to God it was her. He waited and waited but Mina never called.

Mina braced herself as he stepped into her personal space. Victor towered over her. For a brief second, she wanted to lay all their problems down and call a truce. Then she remembered Samia. They couldn't go back. She had to keep pushing forward.

"What you doing here?" Victor asked coldly.

"I wanna be here. Don't act like you ain't wanna see me." She slid her fingertips down the lapel of his jacket. "I see you got yo' bitch workin' for you." She looked over his shoulder at Samia.

"Fuck Samia. You need to be worried about why you kept my son away from me and why you walkin' around here lookin' like Peter Pan and shit." He eyed her hair. "Why the fuck you cut yo' hair?"

"'Cause I wanted to. You know I look good." Mina ran her hand down the back of her head.

"If you say so." Victor played it off.

She did look good, but he'd never tell her that.

"Y'all just one big happy family now, ain't you?" Mina shot mockingly.

"She needed a job to get back on her feet so I hired her."

"How long she been working here?"

Victor looked up at the ceiling. Fighting with Mina was the last thing he wanted to do. He knew as soon as he told her the truth they'd start beefing again.

"Since I bought her back to the United States," he answered truthfully.

"Is that right?" Mina nodded her head, flabbergasted.

With Victor, it was one thing after another. The layers of betrayal just continued to mount. She felt sick to her stomach. Love had escaped her grasp. It was no longer tangible. It was time to get off this psychotic merry-go-round. Mina reached inside her bag. It was clear that she had made the right decision. Delicious, Janiya and Neosha watched their exchange with baited breath.

"Here." She handed him a rolled up stack of papers.

"What is this?" He took the papers from her hand.

"Divorce papers. I want a divorce." She swallowed the lump in her throat.

Victor glared at her.

"I ain't signing this shit." He shook his head disbelievingly.

He was pissed at Mina but divorce was never an option. Victor tried to hand the papers back to her but Mina wouldn't take them.

"I'm not gon' fight with you about this. You made your choice when you continued to lie to me. I'm bowing out gracefully. You and Samia can be together." She bypassed him and stormed off.

Samia stood off in the cut watching their every move. Victor was slipping from her grasp. As soon as they got to the States things between them started to slow down. He hadn't touched her in months. Samia didn't know what she was going to do. Her plan was faltering. If she didn't make a move quick, she was going to lose Victor for good.

Mina didn't know where she was going. She had to get out of there. The walls were starting to close in on her. She desperately needed fresh air. Victor was hot on her trail. There was no way she was going to ask for a divorce and then just leave like she hadn't stabbed him in the chest. They needed to talk about the severity of what was happening. A divorce wouldn't just affect them. The kids would be hysterical.

Outside in the warm, night air, Mina tried to figure out what her next move would be when a familiar face appeared out of nowhere. At first, Mina didn't recognize him. Bishop knew exactly who she was. He'd fantasized about her for weeks. He'd wanted to go back to the shop to check on her but didn't wanna come off like a creep. Like an angel, there she was posted up on the sidewalk.

"Mina, hold up!" Victor came after her.

Not wanting to talk, she waved at the dude. Victor stopped dead in his tracks to see what she was doing. Mina looked over her shoulder at Victor and walked towards the guy. She didn't remember where she knew him from but it didn't matter. She was angry and trying to prove a point to Victor that they were done.

"Hey, baby!" She smiled.

"What's up?" Bishop looked around to make sure she was talking to him.

"Just smile and play along," she whispered.

Bishop looked at her confused for a second but decided he'd grant her request.

"'Bout time you showed up. I've been waiting on you all night." She spoke loudly so Victor could hear.

"My bad, baby. I got caught up. You forgive me?"

"Of course, I do, baby." Mina wrapped her arms around his neck. "My husband is standing right behind us. Is he watching?" She whispered into his ear.

"Mmm hmm." Bishop scooped her up in his arms and kissed her on the neck.

"Good." She closed her eyes and kissed him passionately on the lips.

Victor balled his fist. The thugged-out killer inside of him wanted to fuck Mina and the dude up.

"You want me to handle this, boss?" Tony asked.

"Nah." Victor called off his goon.

There were too many people around for him to cut up. Victor didn't need any heat on him or his organization. A less than smart man would act off emotions. Victor was smarter than that. He was going out of his mind but he refused to let anger and pride cloud his better judgement. Mina had hit him where it hurt. Seeing her kiss another man in his face was like a stab wound to the heart. She'd embarrassed the fuck out of him in front of his people.

If Mina wanted to be petty, then that was all on her. Victor knew how the game went. She wouldn't feel better about herself in the end. After she finished with that nigga, she'd still be in love with him.

"Who the fuck is that my wife wit'?"

He didn't recognize the guy but the gold, Medusa head, pinky ring on his finger looked oddly familiar.

"I don't know, boss. I ain't never seen him around here before."

"Find out who the fuck he is and keep an eye on her." Victor scowled walking back inside.

"I got you, Jefe," Tony confirmed.

For Victor, it had become crystal clear that all of this had happened for a reason. Maybe it was the universe's way of saying things between him and Mina weren't meant to be. She would never be able to put her trust in him again and he was tired of fighting with her on a daily. Where passion end, pain began. They'd started a never-ending cycle of abuse. One moment led to another feud. Things had to end. If Mina wanted a divorce, he was going to give it to her.

"You gon' watch my fat ass twist, boy. As I bounce to the next dick, boy."

-Beyoncé, "Don't Hurt Yourself"

#19

"You probably gon' hate me, but I'm sorry, I don't remember your name," Mina said as Bishop pulled off from the curb.

His Cadillac had a new car smell to it that she loved.

"So you just get in the car wit' muthafuckas you don't know? Let me find out you crazy for real." He joked.

"I swear, I'm not," Mina laughed.

"Yeah, a'ight. That's what all you females say in the beginning. Then you get six months in and find out the chick really is crazy. Be blowin' up yo' phone, slashing your tires and shit."

"That's 'cause you young and probably mess wit' a bunch of baby bitches. When you get my age, you ain't got time for the games." Mina remarked knowing damn well she was crazy as hell.

"How old are you?" Bishop asked.

"I can tell you young. Didn't yo' mama tell you not to ever ask a woman her age?" She playfully hit him in the arm.

"My mother's dead; and I was told that if you want answers you better ask questions."

"I'm sorry to hear that," Mina apologized.

"It's cool. She died when I was a baby. I don't remember her at all." Bishop did 65 down highway 70.

Mina wondered what it would be like not to have a mother. Rita was a handful. Things were still very rocky between them, but Mina wouldn't be able to function without her mother.

"Where we going? You want me to drop you off at the crib?"

"Nigga, you tryin' to get both of us killed? Hell naw, you ain't takin' me home. I still don't even know who I'm in the car with. I remember your face. I just can't place where I know you from."

"That's fucked up. How you gon' forget your future husband's name? I'm Bishop, remember?"

"Yeah!" Mina snapped her finger. "You're the guy from the shop."

Mina took all of him in. *How in the hell could I forget this fine-ass muthafucka,* she thought. Bishop was the truth. His thick beard shined under the moonlight. He had perfect facial features. Everything about him was aesthetically pleasing. The nigga had her feeling things she hadn't felt in years. Visions of him pulling over and taking her from behind filled her head. His cocky swag, and 'I will fuck the shit out of you' good looks, made the heartbeat in her clit thump overtime.

Something about the way he spoke made her want to take it there with him one time, but Mina couldn't let him get the best of her. She had enough drama going on in her life to add fuckin' with some young-ass dude from around the way. It wouldn't be good for either of them. Victor had probably already put a hit out on both their lives after the stunt she pulled. Mina was instantly brought back to reality when the feel of her phone vibrating inside her purse caught her attention.

"Hello?" She answered, imagining his tongue on her clit.

"Where the hell yo' ass go? We been lookin' all over for you!" Delicious yelled into the phone.

"Calm down, Tina Turner. I'm ok. I left with a friend." She gazed over at Bishop who was lighting up a blunt.

Mina wished his lips were wrapped around one of her hard nipples instead.

"Heffa, please, you ain't got no friends besides us."

"You remember the li'l dude from the shop I met a while back?" She turned her head and whispered.

"Yasssssssssssssss! Eyes and nose by Tina Knowles, lips by Denzel, skin from Jesus. Fuck yeah, I remember him. Shit, you done made my dick hard just thinkin' about him."

"I'ma hang up on you," Mina said wanting to throw up.

"Ok, Miss Mina, I see you, girl. A bitch about to get some dick to-night." Delicious stuck out his tongue and cackled. "Don't get nothin' on you, Bernie. Be careful. He look like he got a monster on him. Some of that chocolate cocaine."

"Don't he?" Mina agreed.

"And don't let him hit you with the death stroke. That's what got you fucked up the last time with li'l nacho supreme."

"Shut up. I can't stand you," Mina giggled. "I'll hit you up to let you know I'm ok."

"Alright, girl. Call me if you need backup and make sure you text me that nigga license plate number. His ass fuck around and be a damn serial killer."

"I will." Mina hung up.

Bishop began to play Future's *Rich Sex*.

"So I'm a li'l dude?" He blew a cloud of weed smoke into the air.

"My bad. You just mad younger than me. What you like 26, 28?"

"Mina, I'm probably older than you. I'm 30," Bishop passed her the blunt.

"Get the fuck outta here," Mina said shocked. "You look hella young. You look like a baby." She took a deep pull off the blunt.

"You won't be sayin' that when I put this grown man dick up in you," he challenged.

Caught off guard by his response, Mina held her chest and coughed.

"I am not fuckin' you." She regained her composure.

"Yes you are."

"No, I'm not. I am married." She flashed her ring.

"That don't mean shit to me. You in the car wit' me for a reason. You want me just like I want you." He said, gripping her thigh.

Mina looked down as his strong hand traveled up and down her caramel-colored thigh. The seat of her panties were soaking wet.

"Fall back, bruh." She removed his hand and placed it back on his lap. "You fine as fuck, and if it was 10 years ago, I would take it there with you but I got a lot going on in my life. And my bad for involving you in it. My husband—" Mina cut herself off. "I mean, my soon-to-be ex-husband is a very powerful and dangerous man. I ain't tryin' to get you hurt. I wanna see you live."

Bishop ran his hand down his face and laughed.

"You done?" He asked her.

"Yeah," Mina shrugged.

"A'ight." He took the blunt from her and took another puff. "Ain't nobody trippin' off yo' man. I got mad respect for the big homie, but that nigga old. He washed up—"

"Hold up." Mina stopped him.

"Nah, let me finish. No disrespect, for real."

"You sure?" She spat about to flip.

Victor was on her shit list but she wasn't about to let some nigga she barely knew talk shit about him.

"All I'm sayin' is, life is like a game of chess. A king can't be a king without the strength of his queen, ya dig?"

Mina didn't like him talking about Victor but she couldn't deny the fact that he was tellin' the truth. Victor had disrespected home in a big way and lost the best thing to ever happen to him.

"See, if you was my girl, you would never be put in the position where you had to use another man to make me jealous. I'ma take care of mines. See, ole boy done took his eyes off the prize. You the type of chick that make a nigga wanna settle down and have kids."

"Whoa-whoa-whoa." Mina held up her hand. "You moving way too fast."

"I'm not tryin' to excite you. I'm tryin' to wife you, Bamboo earrings, white Air Nike you," he grinned.

Mina paused. Victor had said the same thing to her back in the day.

"What? You scared? Don't be scared." Bishop held her hand.

"I'm a grown woman. Grown women don't get scared." She laughed, trying her best to seem unaffected by his powerful presence.

"If that's the case, then quit bullshittin' and come home wit me."

Two wrongs didn't make a right, but it damn sure felt good. Mina had no plans on fuckin' Bishop but as they entered the hotel suite, she didn't have any regrets. His Hennessy-soaked tongue was working magic on her pussy. Bishop worked his tongue in and out her honeycomb slit. His face was buried in the folds of her pussy. It had practically disappeared; he was so deep. Mina watched in sheer agony. Bishop was toying with her pussy while flicking his tongue across her clit. Slowly he eased two fingers inside.

"Ooooooooh!" She whimpered.

Bishop took his fingers out and placed them in her mouth so she could taste her juices. Mina licked his fingers clean savoring her strawberry, sticky cream. Loving how nasty she was, Bishop then stuck them back in her slit. Mina's pussy was the sweetest he'd ever tasted. He couldn't get enough of it. It was the perfect shade of pink.

Mina had a body like a pornstar. There wasn't an ounce of cellulite on her. Bishop flipped Mina over onto her stomach. He licked her fat pussy from behind. Mina took one of her nipples in her mouth and sucked. She hadn't envisioned her night ending with her face down and her ass up in the air, but the way Bishop was eating her pussy made her thankful for the decision.

Mina bounced her ass on his face. She was sure to cum if he kept on eating her pussy that way. Mina bit into her lower lip and sat up on all fours. She wanted the D. Bishop took the hint and placed on a condom. His dick was throbbing it was so hard. With the condom on, he slapped Mina on the ass and stuck his dick deep inside.

"Ahhhhhhhhh... yes!" She pinched her nipple.

"Ohhhhh... fuck." He slapped her hard on the ass again.

"Bishop!" Mina wailed.

His dick was so big she felt suffocated.

"I like that dick inside my pussy!" She played with her pussy while he fucked her from behind.

Bishop slammed his cock in and out while gripping her shoulder. Mina's fat ass bounced on his dick. She wished it was Victor fucking her instead. Sex with Bishop was good but it would never compare to the sexual history she had with her husband. Victor knew her body inside and out. Bishop could feel the nut building in the tip of his dick. He didn't want to cum so fast but Mina's pussy felt amazing.

"Shit!" He closed his eyes.

"Mmmmmmm… I'm gonna cum," Mina rotated her fingers faster. "Ahhhhhhhhhh… fuck!" She climaxed wanting to scream out Victor's name.

Accountability:

The quality or state of being accountable.

"You look nothin' like your mother. You look everything like your mother." –Warsan Shire (as heard in Beyoncé's Lemonade)

#20

The afternoon sun peeked through the curtains hanging from the window. The soft amber glow of the sun danced around Mina's face as she gazed at herself in the mirror. She sat perched at her grandmother's old vanity. For years she'd begged her grandmother to give it to her, but Nana Marie always said no but that she could have it when she died. The vanity had been passed down to her from her mother. It was a vintage, aqua dresser and vanity set. A vintage, silver-plated hair brush and comb, antique hand mirror, 1930's, pink, depression, glass perfume bottles and a vintage vanity grooming glass tray decorated the table. The setup was nothing short of exquisite.

Like herself, her grandmother was a lover of beautiful things. When she was younger, Nana Marie was the personification of glamour and class. Mina admired an old picture of her from back in the late 50's. Nana Marie was the shit when she was a young girl. In the picture, her hair was perfectly slicked back in a bun. She had pencil thin, black eyebrows, doe-shaped eyes, ruby red lips, hoop earrings and a backless, floral print top that tied in a bow around the neck.

Mina wished she could be half the woman her grandmother was. Mina looked exactly like her and nothing like her mother. She possessed the same golden skin, round eyes and rose-colored cheeks. Mina studied her own facial features as she got dressed. The silk, spaghetti strap dress she wore clung to her hips and breasts. She was getting ready for a date with Bishop. She'd seen him every day that week. Mina didn't exactly know what she was doing with him but it was fun. With him, she didn't have to think too much. He allowed her the space to live in the moment without putting a label on their friendship.

Mina knew she was out of control and behaving recklessly. She had no business fooling around with Bishop. It was a casual fling on her part that would lead nowhere. She'd never make him her man. He was simply there to fill the void of not having Victor around. She hoped and prayed to God that his feelings weren't getting too deep for her. The last thing she wanted to do was hurt him too. There had been too many causalities already.

Being with Bishop allotted her the opportunity to escape from the troubles of her maddening world. Each day she spent away from her kids wreaked havoc on her conscious. She couldn't face them. It was far easier to run away. Facing Lelah and José would prove that the end was near. How could she look them in the eyes and tell them that the close-knit family they once were was no more? She couldn't break their hearts. Hers still hadn't mended.

Rita opened the door to her mother's bedroom and helped her inside. Dressed in a white duster, Nana Marie walked slowly and sat on the foot of her bed. Three generations of black women sat in one room. Generations of hope, disappointment, anger, pain, resilience, determination and courage ran through each of their veins. Nana Marie had sat back for weeks watching the destruction of her granddaughter without saying a word. She saw her destroying herself.

The fury and bitterness Mina felt seeped through her pores and permeated the entire house. The decisions and choices she was making were life-altering; not only to herself, but to others around her. Nana Marie couldn't take it anymore. The tension between Mina and Rita was unpleasant to be around. Something had to be said.

"Thank you, baby," She said to Rita as she made herself comfortable on the bed.

"You need anything else, Mama?" Rita asked.

"Yeah, for you to have a seat. I wanna talk to the both of you."

"Mama, I told you me and Mina are fine. Now that her eye has healed, she's learned her lesson," Rita glared at her daughter.

"No, you're not fine, so sit yo' butt down," Nana Marie commanded.

"Ma—"

"Don't make me have to tell you again, girl!" Nana Marie said at once.

Rita rolled her eyes and begrudgingly sat down.

"Nana, I would love to sit and talk but I'm on my way out the door," Mina tried to explain.

"You ain't going nowhere today."

"Nana, you can't keep me in the house. I'm a grown woman," Mina chuckled.

"I can't tell. You ain't been actin' like it. Now don't let the old age fool you. I will still take you across my knee." Nana Marie said, not in the mood for games.

Seeing she wasn't playing, Mina sat quiet. She knew not to test her grandmother. Nana Marie looked back and forth at her girls. She desperately wished they both knew how much power they possessed.

"I have lived 91 glorious years. Some days were better than others. I have cried and I have struggled. It took me years before I realized that I could be what I wanted to be without a man. For years, I sat around waiting on your father to return." She stared at Rita.

"I got on my knees, daily, praying to God to send him back to me. I didn't wanna raise two little girls alone. I was trained by my mother to stay with a man I knew was no good, who constantly cheated on me because she was raised to believe that all men lie and cheat. She would say to me through my tears, *"girl, you betta stay with that man. You think you the only woman to ever get cheated on?"* So I did what I was told and ran blind, only to get left in the end anyway. I didn't want to be like my mother; angry, vengeful and bitter. I didn't want to repeat the cycle of the black women in my family who came before me." Nana Marie declared on the verge of tears.

"I wanted to do better by my girls, but when Rita came to me with tears in her eyes telling me what Ed had done, I found myself repeating my mother's words to her. I failed you, honey. I should've taught you better."

Rita sat beside her mother weeping silently. Tears strolled down her face and neck, landing on her fingertips. She'd waited over 30 years for her mother to say this. Mina could count on her hands how many times she'd ever seen her mother cry. Seeing her in tears took Mina out.

"Instead of uplifting you and affirming that you are made of black magic, splendor and wonder, I made you feel like you were the problem. It wasn't your fault. You did nothing wrong. All you did was repeat the pattern that was set before you. We accept so much from our men because we're conditioned to feel unworthy. From the time we're born, we're told our hair isn't good enough, our skin isn't light enough, we're too fat, we're too black, too loud, too aggressive, too tough."

"We're conditioned to think that everything about us is wrong. When we are the salt of the earth. My mother never told me that I didn't have to accept scraps in order to be loved. I was taught to endure heartache with my head held high. Pretend like you don't see lipstick on his collar, ignore the nights he doesn't come home. We put so much into our men 'cause we recognize that they are kings. We see how they are idolized, revered and feared. We coddle them, bathe them in our essence, our blood, sweat and tears and it all goes unnoticed. They don't see how wonderful we are 'cause they feel unworthy too."

Heavy, thick tears flowed from Mina's eyes. She'd never heard any of this from her grandmother. She hated that it had taken 36 years for her to drop such precious jewels. A newfound respect for her grandmother sprouted inside her soul. This was what she needed to hear. All she ever wanted was for someone to recognize her pain. There were so many questions that needed to be answered. Mina was a woman in doubt.

"I hear what you sayin', Nana, but you don't understand." She sat in a heap of tears. "I do everything for that man. I cook, clean, take care of the kids, make sure he's straight, work, try to be cute and docile. I spend so much of my time tryin' to be everything for him that I barely have a minute to breathe."

"Who told you to do all of that?" Nana Marie quizzed.

"Nobody," Mina said feeling dumb. "That's what I saw Mama do."

"Listen, girl, don't you ever bend over backwards for no man. You don't have to prove yourself to nobody. You are good enough, just as you are. Either he loves you or he don't."

"Nobody ever taught me how to be a wife. The only thing Mama said to me was be self-sufficient, don't let no man hit on you and that I'll never have to worry about anything financially with Victor but that I'll have to share him with other women if I chose to marry him."

"See... this is why I wanted to talk to both of you. This cycle... this generational curse on our family is going to stop here today!" Nana Marie declared. "Let me tell you something, Mina. Men are simple. All they want is food, sex and their ego stroked. You have to let a man lead. You are not the man in the relationship. Victor is, so let him be. You sittin' up here tryin' to be Wonder Woman when you don't have to be. Let him be the hunter and the provider. A man just wants to feel needed; that's all. That don't mean that you have to accept anything he gives you. It's not ok for a man to cheat on you."

"I'm sorry, Fat Mama," Rita gazed tearfully in her daughter's eyes. "I didn't know no better. All these years, I've been tryin' to hide the pain I felt when I found out your dad got another woman pregnant. I didn't want to lose my family or my man, so I sucked it up and pretended that everything was ok. I didn't want Ann to think she'd won. Boy, was I dumb. I lost anyway. I lost the minute I decided to stay with your father without him facing the repercussions of his ways. Here I was, lost and broken, and he went on with life as if my heart wasn't laid out on the floor. He never suffered," Rita heaved becoming infuriated.

"He didn't care that he'd destroyed me." She rose to her feet.

Mina saw the fury in her mother's eyes. She knew it like she knew the back of her hand. She'd seen it in her own eyes. All of Mina's life, she thought her and her mother didn't have anything in common. They didn't look alike, act alike, talk alike, dress alike or behave alike. Now she realized that they were more alike than she thought. She was just like her mother. Everything she hated about Rita, she disliked about herself. They both walked around faking strength, when on the real, they were dying inside. Both women hid behind hair, makeup and clothes so that no one could see the window to their soul. Now that the veil had come down, Mina found herself feeling closer to her mother.

"Mama, calm down," she urged.

"That big head muthafucka gotta die!" Rita ran out of the room.

"See, Nana, look what you done!" Mina chased after her mother.

"I got some bail money in my purse." Nana Marie laid down, unfazed.

Ed needed his ass kicked. It had been 30 years overdue.

"Ed! Where are you?!" Rita raced through the house.

"I'm out here, suga foot!" Ed shouted from the front yard.

Rita pushed open the screen door and found her husband sitting on the lawn couch with his boxers and cowboy boots on. He was living the good life. Ed didn't have a care in the world. He sat basking in the sun, sipping on a homemade Pina Colada. He even had the nerve to have a straw umbrella in his drink. Seeing him so relaxed pissed Rita off even more. She turned the water on and grabbed the hose.

"Mama, no!" Mina yelled from the front porch.

"Hush up, girl!" Rita stormed over to where her husband was.

"What it do, suga lump? Come sit on Daddy lap." He turned and looked at her.

"Sitting on Daddy's lap is what got Ann pregnant!" She turned the hose on him.

"What the hell?" Ed tried to block the water to no avail. "Woman, what is wrong wit' you?"

"You! You hurt me! You let me down, Ed!" She continued to douse him with the hose. "Why'd you cheat on me, man? I loved you!"

"What you talkin' about? That happened over 30 years ago!" Ed slipped off the couch, trying not to drown.

"And 30 years later, you still don't understand what you done to me! I am half the woman I used to be, Ed!"

"Well actually…" He looked over her body.

Rita was bigger than the woman she used to be.

"Oh no the hell you didn't! You tryin' to call me fat!" Rita shrieked pressing the nozzle down harder.

Mina held her head down in embarrassment. Several of her parents' white neighbors were outside watching the whole ordeal.

"I'm sorry, baby! Just please! Don't kill me!" Ed flopped around the grass like a fish. "I love you! Lord knows I do! You the moon to my stars! The Blue to my Magic. The chicken to my grease! Just please, baby! Don't kill me!"

"Somebody gon' die tonight and it sure as hell ain't gon' be me!" Rita hissed.

"Oh, Lord! I can't breathe!" Ed rolled around the grass trying to dodge the water. "Elizabeth, is that you?" He quoted Sanford and Son.

"I'm coming! Lord, I see the light! Somebody help me! Please!"

"But you caught up in your permanent emotions."

-Beyoncé, "Love Drought"

#21

August was here. It was the last day of summer camp for José. On the last day, each year, was the camp's annual talent show. The kids had all summer to practice and perfect their routine. The kids could dance, sing, play an instrument, act, whatever; as long as they had the courage to get up in front of their peers and parents to perform. The staff even participated.

José took the talent show very serious. Each year he showcased a different talent or trick. One year he did a magic show that didn't turn out so well. When it was time for him to pull the rabbit out of the hat, he learned that the rabbit had suffocated and died. For a year straight, José wouldn't look at a rabbit or go near a carrot. The following year, he took it upon himself after watching Electric Boogaloo to breakdance - which was a complete disaster. Everything was going great until he tried to do the robot and landed on his head with a concussion.

Mina couldn't believe he got a concussion from doing the robot! Like, how does that happen? After that fiasco, Mina forbid him to breakdance ever again. José refused to give up. He was a fighter just like his mother and father. He was determined to beat his nemesis, Aaron. Aaron won first place year after year. José was sick of it. This was going to be his year to take home the trophy. That year, he had a secret weapon. The other kids wouldn't be competition at all.

Mina showed up with her entire family and the staff from the shop. She wasn't going to miss José's performance for the world. After the long talk she had with her grandmother and mother, Mina started to feel like her old self again. Waking up alone wasn't so bad anymore. She no longer felt like she was sentenced to death. She hadn't fully healed, but she was on her way there. Mina got out her car and watched as her father got out his van and stretched. He'd been in the dog house since Rita ran up on him with the water hose.

Ed wasn't allowed to sleep in their room. He'd been banished to the couch for over a week. He'd tried everything to get back in her good graces. He tried giving her chocolates, flowers, bottles of Yak, bundles of weave but nothing worked. Rita was going to make him pay for the turmoil he put her through. Mina felt bad for her dad but he had to learn that a scorned woman wasn't to be played with.

Rita, Aunt Bernice and Nana Marie had left a half hour early and were already there. Mina was so happy that her grandmother was getting out of the house. She needed some fresh air. Uncle Chester and Smokey weren't far behind them.

Mina inhaled deeply. It would be the first time she saw Victor since the club. Victor hadn't signed the divorce papers, so she didn't know how he felt about her or where he stood when it came to their relationship. She also hadn't seen Lelah or José in weeks. She'd been racking her brain for days on how she was going to approach them.

Nervous butterflies filled the pit of her stomach as they entered the gymnasium. A big, black curtain stretched across the stage with a banner that read: Summer Camp Talent Show. Pictures of the kids and gold, hanging stars hung from the ceiling. Tons of families were there. Mina waved at a few of the parents she knew. She was causally cute in a light grey, fitted tank, body-hugging, beige, ankle-length midi skirt and all-white Adidas. Three, delicate, gold necklaces and a Cartier gold watch was the only jewelry she wore.

Mina didn't even have her wedding ring on. Wearing it didn't feel right to her anymore. She didn't know how Victor would feel seeing her without it. She couldn't go around worrying about what would make Victor upset. Her grandmother was right. She had to worry about herself and put her needs first. Mina was done trying to be his Super Woman. She wasn't Karen White.

"Eww... I can feel me gettin' sick already." Delicious held his nose.

"What are you talkin' about? We just got here?" Mo quizzed, rubbing her stomach.

It had gotten even bigger.

"All these li'l snotty nose kids. They give me the hebegebees. You can't tell me one of them ain't got the Ebola virus," he coughed. "See! My throat starting to itch already! Oh, Lord, I'm about to die. Jesus, take the wheel!"

"Boy, if you don't hush! Ain't nobody got time for yo' foolishness today," Jodie sneered. "You know, James Chapter 5 verse 15 says and the prayer of faith shall save the sick, and the Lord shall raise him up; and if he have committed sins, they shall be forgiven him."

"What the hell does that mean?" Delicious placed his hand on his hip.

"I rebuke that sick demon in the name of the Jesus." Jodie smacked him on the forehead like the preachers do in church. "Now shut the hell up, Purvis Elroy the third," Jodie called Delicious by his government name.

"Don't you ever say my name out in public." He looked around frantically. "You know I'm wanted in all 50 states."

"Y'all done made my asshole hurt." Mo groaned.

"That's her. She's the one distracting me from all these sexy daddies up in here. Somebody about to get they man took to-night! I'm glad I bought this extra box of Fleet," Delicious stuck out his tongue.

"You have no shame, do you?" Jodie frowned.

"Nope, and if you keep on talkin', I'ma sit on yo' man dick too." Delicious tapped the tip of her nose with his finger.

"Die! Satan, die!" Jodie flicked him with her travel size bottle of bless oil.

"Stop! You gon' ruin my outfit!" He tried to run away. "You know you can't get oil stains out of rayon!"

"Will y'all act like adults for like five seconds?" Mina requested, a nervous wreck.

She was trying to locate the kids and her family. She didn't see her mother, granny or aunt anywhere.

"Mom!" Lelah jumped up from her seat, waving her arms from side to side.

Mina's eyes lit up as soon as she saw her daughter. She knew that seeing Lelah would be emotional but she hadn't expected a rush of emotions to sweep over her. Being away from her kids for so long had been one of the dumbest and most rewarding things she'd ever done. She'd learned a lot about herself and her family while away.

"Babygirl!" Mina wrapped Lelah up in her arms. "I missed you." She squeezed her tight.

"Here, I bought you these." Mina handed her a bouquet of flowers.

"Mom, you didn't have to do that." Lelah said sincerely. "Seeing you is enough for me. I've missed you like crazy." She hugged her again.

"The house isn't the same without you there."

"I haven't been the same without you guys. You've been holding the fort down while I've been away?"

"Yeah." Lelah nodded. "Mom, can I talk to you alone for a second?"

"Sure, love."

Lelah and Mina stepped off to the side.

"Mom, I want you to know that I understand why you've been gone. You and Dad are going through a lot. I know it hasn't been easy for you to have my other mother back. But you gotta understand, I love you. You're my mom. Nobody is ever going to take your place in my life. Outside of Granny Faith, you're the only mother I know."

Tears flooded Mina's eyes but she swore she wasn't going to cry.

"I'm not going to mess up my makeup." She fanned her face.

"You bet not 'cause you are beat, honey!" Lelah snapped her finger. "But for real, I love you, Mom."

"I love you too." Mina held her daughter close. "Where's your father? Is he here?" She looked around the gym.

"Yeah, he's right over there." Lelah pointed to the stands.

Victor sat facing the stage on his phone.

"C'mon." Lelah took her mother's hand. "The show is about to start. Let's go take our seats."

"I don't think I should sit in the same area as your father. I don't think that's such a good idea," Mina hesitated.

"Mom, c'mon. I'm not taking no for an answer." Lelah pulled her into the bleachers.

Mina and the crew sat on the same row as Victor. After speaking to everyone except Mina, he went back to playing Candy Crush on his phone. Victor had no plans of even acknowledging Mina's presence. He was done with her. She'd disrespected him in the worst possible way. There was no coming back from kissing another man in his face. He didn't give a fuck how mad she was. Plus, she didn't have a wedding ring on. Victor was her and her shenanigans.

Mina pretended like she wasn't bothered that he didn't speak but deep down her feelings were hurt. She couldn't say she didn't deserve his silent treatment. What she did was foul as fuck, but Victor deserved a taste of his own medicine. It was funny that he could fuck a whole other bitch, but as soon as she repaid the favor, she became the villain.

Victor was supposed to be this tough, macho guy. He wore his pride like a badge of honor. When he was pissed, there was no getting through to him. As far as Mina was concerned, he could stay mad. She didn't care. They'd become public enemies. At least that's what she tried to tell herself. Throughout the show, she kept looking at him out of the corner of her eye. Victor was far too fine of a man to ignore.

Just being in his presence turned Mina on. She missed the taste of his skin on her tongue. She was addicted to him. No other man would be able to satisfy her like he could. He knew exactly which buttons to push to send her over the edge. The way his long cock used to slide in and out of her wet slit used to send her into a tailspin. She couldn't let him go.

Victor felt her eyes on him. He wasn't going to give her the satisfaction of giving her eye contact. Mina had dug her grave. It was time for her to lay in it. There would be no more back and forth. There used to be a time when he would rather argue with her than be with someone else. Now, he'd rather be by his fuckin' self. He was tired of playing the blame game. They'd both done their dirt. Neither of them could take back their transgressions. It was all set in stone.

He refused to let her see him get emotional. Even though it tore him up to hear about her running around with another nigga like she wasn't his wife, Victor couldn't sweat it none. He knew she wasn't gettin' the type of pipe he used to give her from that li'l bum-ass dude.

They were so far gone from the people they used to be. Mina wasn't the same woman he married. He was partially to blame for that. He'd changed her for the worse.

Halfway through the show, it was time for José to take the stage. Mina stood on her feet and cheered. She was so excited to see her baby perform. She didn't know what kind of performance he'd put together. Her and the entire family stood with baited breath as the curtains drew back and the lights came up. Suddenly, her mother walked on the stage dressed like Dr. Dre during his NWA days. Rita had on a L.A. cap, gold, rope chain and an all-black Dickie suit. The crowd went silent. Rita put the mic up to her lips and said:

"Ay yo, Eazy? Why don't you come from out the piano and bust this crazy shit?"

José stepped to the center of the stage wearing a black baseball cap with the words Compton written across it. A Jerry curl wig peeked out from underneath. He wore a black windbreaker buttoned all the way up, a gold, cross chain, black jeans and a fresh pair of Dope Man Nikes. With the mic in his hand, he looked at the crowd and started rapping as the beat dropped:

"Woke up quick at about noon,

Just thought that I had to be in Compton soon,

I gotta get drunk before the day begins,

Before my mother start bitchin' about my friends."

Mina's mouth flew open. There her 10-year-old son was, performing NWA's *Boyz 'n Da Hood* with his grandmother, Aunt Bernice and Nana Marie. Aunt Bernice hyped the crowd up in a Raiders jacket and hat like she was Ice Cube. Nana Marie was on the ones and twos pretending to be DJ Yella. She had on a NWA snapback, gold chain and a white, velour, jogging suit. Mina was outdone.

All the white folks in the audience were appalled. They covered their children's ears and shook their heads in disapproval. They couldn't believe that any parent would allow their child to listen to such crude music and display such vulgar behavior. After the initial shock wore off, Mina and her family got their whole entire life. They all cheered José, Rita, Aunt Bernice and Nana Marie on. Victor couldn't have been prouder of his son. He was ripping the stage. He had all of Eazy E's mannerisms down pat.

"Cruising down the street in my 6-4

Jockin' the freaks, clocking the dough

Went to the park to get the scoop

Knuckleheads out there cold shooting some hoops," José Crip walked across the stage.

Mina was amped as hell. Her baby was doing the damn thing. She didn't give a fuck what the other parents thought. This was hip hop at its finest. To see her son on stage with his granny and great-grandmother was an absolute delight. Mina couldn't believe that Nana Marie had been planning to participate the entire time.

"'Cause the boyz n tha hood are always hard

You come talking that trash we'll pull your card

Knowing nothing in life but to be legit

Don't quote me, boy, 'cause I ain't said shit!" José grabbed his dick then put his middle finger in the air before dropping the microphone.

Mina and Victor clapped so hard their hands became sore. Needless to say, José didn't win the talent show. For once, he didn't care. The joy of performing a hip hop classic with the women he loved meant more to him than a stupid trophy.

"Baby, you did so good!" Mina kissed his chubby cheeks repeatedly.

"Stop, Mom, you're embarrassing me." He scrunched up his face.

José wouldn't dare admit it, but he secretly loved his mother's kisses.

"I'm so proud of you."

"Thanks." José fixed his clothes.

"I'm sorry, again, about what happened. I didn't mean a word I said. You know that, right?" Mina apologized. "I plead temporary insanity." She held her hand up.

"I know. I forgive you." José gave his mom a quick hug. "Does that mean now you're coming home?"

"You did the damn thing, son." Victor came up and gave him a five before Mina could reply.

"Thanks, Pop." José smiled, pleased with himself. "Mom might be coming home," He said enthusiastically.

"Is that right?" Victor gave Mina the stink eye. "Let me holla at you for a second."

Mina reluctantly followed Victor out into the hall. She hoped and prayed to God he wasn't about to start a fight. Nothing or no one was going to kill her vibe.

"I didn't tell him that I was coming home, if that's what you wanna know." She spat before he got a word out.

"You still fuckin' wit' that nigga?"

Mina stood silent, taken aback.

"You still fuckin' wit' that bitch?" She snapped.

"Answer the question." Victor said sternly.

"Why you worried about what I do?"

"I'm not. 'Cause I know when you layin' wit' that nigga you thinkin' about me." Victor bit his bottom lip aggressively.

"Boy, please. Get over yourself." Mina waved him off.

"Tell me that the pussy ain't mine no more." He got in her face.

Mina stepped back in distress. Only Victor could make her pussy cream with only a few words.

"Tell me you moving on and you don't love me no more," he challenged.

"Back up off me." She pushed him away, flustered. "What I do is none of your business."

"Did you fuck him?" He shot her a look that could kill.

"I don't think you want me to answer that." Mina folded her arms across her chest.

Victor's heart sank down to his toes. She'd actually fucked another nigga.

"Oh word? That's how you feel?"

Mina bit her bottom lip. She had to keep up her strong face. She couldn't be weak.

"Yep."

A million words wanted to escape from Victor's mouth, but his pride wouldn't let him break down and show her how he was really feeling.

"A'ight then." He reached inside his back pocket. "Here." He handed her the divorce papers.

Mina flipped the papers open to the last page. He'd signed them.

"You got what you wanted. I hope you're happy now." Victor looked at her one last time and then walked away.

"You can't recreate her."

-Beyoncé, "Don't Hurt Yourself"

#22

Bryson Tiller's *Don't* bumped as Victor pulled up to Samia's place. He'd put her up in one of the lofts he owned. The place was dope. There was an open floorplan with large living spaces that had plenty of light, natural timber posts, polished concrete floors and exposed brick - for a true loft experience. Samia's master bedroom suite had a customized walk-in closet, large bathroom with double sinks, soaking tub and an open, walk-in, seamless glass shower. She also had an updated kitchen with solid maple cabinetry, stainless steel appliances/backsplash and center island. The in-unit laundry, full guest bath and extra storage on the same floor was a plus.

Samia asked that he come over and help her unclog the tub. Victor told her to call the maintenance man but Samia insisted that he come instead. Playing the role of a plumber wasn't on his list of things to do that day, but since it was Samia, he decided to make the time. Victor was just about to use his key to unlock the door when she pulled it open.

"Thank God, you're here." Samia said wrapped in a towel. "I was just about to get in the shower when the tub started flooding on me."

"Is that right?" Victor smirked.

He was a very good reader of women. He knew Samia was setting a thirst trap. It had been months since he fucked her. Homegirl wanted the D bad. She was constantly trying to throw the pussy at him, but being with Samia sexually wasn't where his head was at anymore. He'd made the decision that fuckin' with her on a relationship-type level wasn't an option. His heart just wasn't there. He would take care of her financially and provide her with anything she needed, but sooner than later, they would have to deal with the legality of their situation. He didn't want to be married to her anymore. Samia was strictly just the mother of his child. Despite the problems he and Mina were going through, Mina had his heart and always would.

Victor came in and placed his red Supreme jacket on the back of one of the dining room chairs. He was determined to stay focused on the task at hand. Samia was making it quite difficult though. Her supple breasts, round behind and smooth legs were an eyeful. All she had to do was drop her hand and her entire body would be on full display.

"It's so hot in here." She fanned her face with her hand. "Aren't you hot?" She asked using her sexy voice.

"Nah, I'm good. Which tub backed up?" Victor asked.

He wanted to fix the drain and get the fuck outta there as quickly as possible.

"The one in the master bedroom." Samia led him to her room.

Victor tried not to look but the way her ass cheeks bounced every time she took a step made his dick jump inside his pants. Samia was not playing fair. When they got in the room, she completely flipped the script on him. Samia did exactly what Victor thought she was going to do. She turned around and let the towel drop to the floor. Her tits and the face of her perfectly, pink pussy were out for him to see. Samia's body was banging. Everything was firm and in place.

"You like?" She shook back her hair and gazed at him provocatively. "You never saw me like this before, huh? We missed you." She purred, referring to her pussy.

"You wild than a muthafucka." Victor tried to keep his cool.

"Don't act like you don't miss us." Samia stepped into his personal space.

Her breasts were pressed up against his broad chest.

"I want you." She softly kissed his lips. "Tell me you don't want me too."

Victor tried his best to fight her advances but his will power was weak as hell. All of the blood in his body had gone to his dick. Sex with Samia was always the best. The things she knew how to do with her tongue would put Karrine Steffens to shame. Before Victor knew it, they were on the bed ravishing one another. Her tongue was down his throat as he gripped her ass. He wanted to fuck her so bad.

"What about the drain? I thought your tub was clogged up?" He asked in-between kisses.

"I am the tub." Samia placed a trail of sensual kisses down his stomach.

His rock-hard abs were like mountain peaks against the taste buds of her tongue. Victor held his head back in anticipation of her sucking his dick. Samia had him right where she wanted. Victor's eyes were closed. Now that she had him distracted, Samia slowly eased her hand underneath the pillow. The nickel-plated 9mm was only inches away.

Then it dawned on Victor. Fucking Samia would only cause more confusion. He had love for her but he wasn't in love with her. The love they once shared was dead and gone. For a minute there, his vision was cloudy. He thought that her returning was a sign from God that with her was where he needed to be. He quickly realized that wasn't true. He wasn't the same young boy he once was.

He was a grown man with a wife he loved tremendously. Mina and the kids were his foundation. The last 10 years of his life with Mina could never be duplicated or replaced. He could never recreate the moments they shared with another woman. No matter how pretty she was or how good the sex was, Samia could never replace Mina.

"Yo, we gotta stop." He abruptly stopped kissing her.

"Why?" She swiftly snatched back her hand.

"This ain't right."

"What you mean it ain't right? Stop fighting this. We love each other, remember?" Samia unbuckled his jeans. "Let me make you feel good." She massaged his penis.

"Fuck," Victor groaned as she licked the tip of his dick.

Samia was just about to put it in her mouth and reach for the gun when he stopped her again.

"Nah, chill." He pushed her off of him.

"What is wrong with you? I thought you said you loved me?" Samia pushed him back down and straddled his lap.

"I do, but not the way you want me to." Victor said honestly.

"Bullshit. You love me. She will never make you feel the way I do. You will always search for me in her." She leaned forward to kiss him as his phone began to ring.

From the sound of the ringtone, Victor knew it was Mina calling.

"Raise up." He pushed Samia all the way off his lap. "Hello?" He answered the call on the second ring.

"Victor!" Mina said in a panic.

"What? What is it?" He asked hearing the desperation in her voice.

Mina was crying hysterically.

"It's Nana Marie. She's dead!"

"Damn," Victor's heart dropped. "A'ight, here I come. Where you at?"

"At my mama's house."

"A'ight, I'll be there in a second." He ended the call. "I gotta go."

As soon as he got up, Samia tried to make a dash for the gun but accidently pushed it behind the bed. Nervous energy swept over her body. If Victor caught on to what she was up to, she'd be dead for sure. Thankfully, she had carpeted floors so Victor didn't hear the gun fall.

"Where you going?" Samia played it off as he turned around.

"To my wife." He quickly zipped up his jeans. "Mina's grandmother passed."

His wife, Samia thought. *That bitch wasn't your wife a second ago when I almost had your dick in my mouth.*

"I'm sorry to hear that." She said instead.

Samia tried to sound compassionate, although she could really give a damn. She didn't give a fuck about Mina or her dead-ass grandma.

"I'll holla at you later." Victor pocketed his phone and raced out the door.

Pissed, Samia hopped off the bed and grabbed her silk robe. Once again, she'd missed the perfect opportunity to get rid of Victor. Now she would have to setup another scenario where she could get him alone. Before Victor got to his car, he realized he left without grabbing his jacket. He was just about to open the door when he overheard Samia on speakerphone.

"Is it done?" The man on the other end asked.

"No! I dropped the gun behind the bed and the bitch's grandmother died so he ran up out of here. Oh my

God, he's such a li'l bitch. I can't stand him! I just want him to die already," she groaned.

"In due time, sweetheart. Just stay cool. Keep making him think you're in love with him and that you want your family back."

"Diego, I can't believe this dumb muthafucka actually thinks I was just stranded in Columbia all these years. He has no idea that I faked the entire thing," she laughed.

"Keep playin' on his emotions. No one can ever know that you were in on murdering your family and that you faked your death. Once Victor is dead, you'll be able to take over the organization. Mina has no claim to the empire 'cause she's not legally his wife. We'll have the Saldono Nation, Cali and the Gonzalez cartel under our belts. No one will be able to fuck with us. We'll have the biggest drug cartel in the world." Diego exclaimed.

"I can't wait. I just hate being away from you." Samia said sweetly into the phone. "I hate that I have to keep throwing myself at him. I didn't like him then and I don't like him now. You're the love of my life. That's why I'm risking it all for you. I never wanted to marry Victor but my stupid father insisted that I marry him. I hated my father for what he did to me. For years he molested me then had the nerve to marry me off to one of his friends' sons like I was a piece of meat. I had to kill him. He had to pay for what he did to me." She seethed with anger.

"It's all good. That's all over now." Diego calmed her down.

"You were right. Marrying Victor and faking my death has proven to be very beneficial."

"When Victor is six feet in the ground, we can finally legally get married and be together forever," Diego professed.

Samia smiled a mile wide.

"Mrs. Samia Vasquez does have a nice ring to it," she beamed.

Victor stood outside the door stunned. His blood was boiling. Samia had her entire family murdered, faked her own death and was plotting to kill him so she could have the corner on all the major cartels. It fucked Victor up even more to know she'd plotted the murder of her family with the very people who had killed them. She sat at the funerals of her mother and father weeping like she was really in mourning. The woman was sick. Victor couldn't believe he'd fallen for her lies and her tears. Now that he knew that she and the son of Ángel Ayala-Vazquez were out to take him down, it was time for Victor to go into murder mode.

Reformation:

The action or process of reforming an institution or practice.

"Trade your broken wings for mine."

-Beyoncé, "All Night Long"

#23

New Northside Baptist Church was packed to capacity. Nana Marie's family came near and far to pay their respects. Members of the family from Arkansas, Alabama and Mississippi where there mourning her death. Everybody from the old neighborhood was at the funeral. Mina was barely able to make it through the service. She was a complete mess. Nana Marie's death had really done a number on her mental state.

Once again, she'd lost a piece of her. This time, she had no way of getting it back. Nana Marie had gone home to the Lord. The only satisfying part of her death was that she had died in her sleep. Everyone sat in the pews dressed in black. It was hotter than fish grease inside the church. Several fans were on but they were only blowing out hot air. Grief mixed with heat made Mina even more upset. Her mother had fell out crying three times and the service wasn't even halfway through yet.

Mina didn't think she was going to make it through the entire funeral service. The wails from her mother's throat caused her to cry harder. Victor sat beside her, holding her in his arms. There was no way he was going to let her go through this alone. She was his family. It didn't matter that divorce was on the table. He was going to be there for her no matter what. She would do the same for him.

He needed to be there for her and the kids too. This was the first time they'd experienced the death of a loved one. Lelah and José couldn't stop crying. Losing Nana Marie was an unbearable experience for the both of them. They didn't know how they'd go on without her. Mina was barely holding on. When Aunt Bernice stood up and started saying her eulogy, she really broke down.

Aunt Bernice started off slow and steady. The longer she spoke, the more she caught the Holy Spirit. Rocking a black and white ladies' church hat, black blazer trimmed in rhinestone, black pencil skirt, stockings and gloves, she walked back and forth across the pulpit. Aunt Bernice was catching the Holy Ghost. Everyone in the room could feel it too. They were all up on their feet clapping and praising the Lord.

"Goodnight, Mama! You left me! But one of these old mornings… I don't know when… oooh... one of these old mornings! I don't know what time! But when God step out! One foot on the land… One on the sea… One of these old days! He gon' blow that horn! Ahhhhhhhhhhhh!" She shouted, waving her hand in the air.

"I'm gon' see you again!" Aunt Bernice fell down to her knees in tears.

Uncle Chester rushed over to her side to help her off the ground.

"Hallelujah!" She yelled as he cooled her off with a church hand fan.

A praise break had broken out. The drummer and organ player played shouting music as everybody danced in their seats. When everyone settled, the preacher spoke, then Mina was asked to come up and sing. Mina was hardly able to stand up on her two feet. She'd never been so weak before. Victor helped her up to the pulpit.

Mina stood in front of the congregation, her parents, Victor, the kids, Mo, Boss and the staff. She hadn't sung in front of a group of people in years. Only Nana Marie could get her to sing again. Mina struggled to find the words. Her heart was so heavy. After two failed attempts, she was finally able to speak. Tears streamed down her face as she sang:

"For allllllllllllllllll weeeee knooooooooooooow,

We may never meeeeeet agaaaaaaaaaaaaaaain,

Befooooooore you gooooooooooooooooo make this moment sweeeeet again,

We won't say gooooodnight untiiiiiiiiiil the last minuuuuuute."

By the time she was done singing, the entire church was in a state of hysteria. Everyone was hootin' and hollerin'. Mina was overjoyed when the whole thing was over. She and Victor stood outside the church holding hands. He hadn't let her go the whole time. Mina needed and appreciated his support. She understood that him being there for her didn't change anything about the state of their relationship. She was just happy he was there. All of the immediate family and friends were headed to Rita's house for the repast. Nana Marie would be cremated the following day.

"How you doing, Fat Mama?" Ed asked cautiously.

He knew his daughter was in a fragile state.

"As good as can be, I guess." Mina hugged her father.

"Vic, come holla at ya boy for a second." Ed pulled him away.

"Yes, sir?"

"Thanks for being here for my daughter, Vic," Ed shook his hand.

"Of course. There's no other place I'd rather be," he assured.

"Listen, son, I know y'all going through some thangs. And I try to stay out of grown folk's business but… she lost her husband, her family and a baby, Vic. You just can't act like that didn't happen."

"I don't. I lost a baby too."

"And you took your grief and you channeled it into another woman. You willed yourself forward into something new and fresh. But Fat Mama she just… I don't know. My baby girl ain't the same no more. But you gotta be there for her." Ed poked his finger into Victor's chest. "Don't do what I did and run away. It don't get you nowhere. Trust me. I'm still suffering for my mistakes 30 years later."

"What if she doesn't come out of it? What if I can't bring her back?" Victor's voice cracked.

"You will. You just gotta have faith." Ed patted him on the arm.

Victor let his father-in-law's words sink in. He was right. He had to step up and be the man his wife needed him to be. He'd given her a million reasons to walk away. Now it was time for him to give her a million reasons to stay. With time, prayer and patience, they could build a home with each other again.

"Y'all ridin' in the limo?" Ed asked Mina.

"Nah, I'ma ride to the house with Victor and the kids," she responded.

"Ok, we'll see y'all there." Ed walked down the steps.

"Speaking of the kids, where are they?" Victor asked.

"The last time I saw them, they were inside the church with Nay's kids." Mina wiped a bead of sweat from her brow.

"A'ight, I'm about to go get 'em. I'll be right back."
Victor walked back inside.

Mina awaited his return when she spotted Bishop
pull up in front of the church. *What the hell is he doing
here,* she thought. She hadn't invited him. Mina didn't want
any problems. She and Victor were finally able to be
around each other without killing one another. She hated
that it had to take Nana Marie dying for them to wave the
white flag. At the end of the day, family came first. Victor
would always be the one she ran to when times got rough.

Bishop hopped out the whip dressed in a navy
Ermenegildo Zegna, tic woven, two-button suit. She'd
never seen him look so sophisticated and dapper. Bishop
approached her with a bouquet of yellow roses in hand.
Mina wanted to bend over and puke. She did not need the
drama of him being there right now.

"Hey." She spoke wearily. "What are you doing
here?"

"I just wanted to check on you and make sure you
was good." He handed her the flowers.

"Thank you. I appreciate it, but... umm..." She
looked over her shoulder to see if the coast was clear. "You

shouldn't be here. My kids and my husband are here and I'm not tryin' to upset my kids any more than they already are. It's just not a good look."

"I feel you. You're very important to me, though. I wouldn't have felt right if I didn't know you were straight." He caressed her cheek.

"Thank you, but I just think me and you need to fall back for a minute."

"Why? You and ole boy gettin' back together?"

"No, this has nothing to do with him. It has everything to do with me. I should've never started messing with you in the first place. I need to clean up my personal life before I start dealing with anybody."

"That's what's up." Bishop nodded as Victor and the kids appeared. "I understand."

Victor ice-grilled Mina and Bishop. He couldn't believe she'd invited him knowing he would be there. Mina had taken disrespect to a whole new level. He didn't give a damn about it being Nana Marie's funeral. Victor was about to bust her ass.

"Y'all go get in the car." He told the kids.

Once they disappeared down the steps, he glared at Mina.

"You wanna introduce me to your friend?"

Mina damn near shit her pants.

"Uhhhh… Victor, this is Bishop. Bishop, this is Victor." She introduced them both.

"What up, OG?" Bishop held up his hand for a pound.

Victor shot him a look of annoyance. Bishop was out of his mind if he thought he was going to get a handshake from Victor. The nigga was dumber than he looked. Bishop quickly realized that Victor was leaving him hanging and lowered his hand. As his hand went back down to his side, Victor noticed his pinky ring again. The ring stuck out to him like a sore thumb.

Where do I know that ring from, he thought. Abruptly, Victor remembered. The gold, Medusa head, pinky ring Bishop was wearing was the same ring the old head, Ángel Ayala-Vazquez, used to wear. Each of his sons were given the same rings at the age of 13. Victor put two and two together and realized that Bishop wasn't this cat's

real name. The muthafucka standing before him was Diego
Vasquez.

"I break chains all by myself."

-Beyoncé, "Freedom"

#24

Two days had passed since Nana Marie's funeral. Mina thought drowning herself in her work would be the perfect remedy to heal her blues. Mina was so tired of feeling sad. The shit seemed to be never-ending. The only thing that made her feel better was knowing that she would be returning home that night to her kids. After the funeral, Victor insisted that she come home. She sensed something was bothering him but didn't want to press the issue.

She was just happy he wanted her home. She missed her house, her kids and her bed. She and Victor hadn't made any plans on reconciling. Mina was cool with that. Fixing their broken relationship was the last thing on her mind. Her main concern was her kids. She needed them more than ever now. It would take months for her to heal from everything that had gone on, plus Nana Marie's sudden death. She couldn't wait to see the surprised look on their faces when they came home Sunday morning and found her there.

Alone, Mina grabbed her purse and began to turn off all the lights. It was pitch black outside. The moon was out. Mina was tired as hell. It was Friday and she'd been at the shop all day. Her back and feet were killing her. Walking around in 4-inch heels for 10 hours straight did a number on the balls of her feet. Mina was just about to turn off the last light when she heard someone walk through the shop's door.

"I'm sorry, we're closed." She said about to turn around.

"No, you're a dead woman, bitch." Samia grabbed her by the back of her head and dragged her down to the ground.

Mina tried to grasp her hands but Samia's grip on her hair was too tight. She was pulling it from the root. Mina just knew she was going to have a bald spot in the back of her head. She tried to break away but the strap of her Chanel purse was tangled around her arm. Samia drug her across the floor. When she finally let her go, she took her pointed-toe shoe and kicked Mina in her ribs.

"Aghhhhhhh!" Mina clutched her side.

"I see you ain't talkin' shit now, bitch!" Samia kicked her in the face.

Blood gushed out of Mina's mouth. She was so caught off guard, she couldn't think straight.

"I thought you was gon' whoop my ass! You talked all that shit! Look at you now!" Samia lifted her leg to kick her again.

Mina caught her foot and pushed her down. Back up on her feet, she regained her composure. She didn't hesitate to do exactly what she promised Samia she was going to do. Mina balled up her fist and punched her square in the pussy.

"I told you not to fuck with me, bitch!" Mina grabbed Samia by the throat.

She tried to choke the life out of her. Mina didn't even know what had brought on this attack.

"Let me go," Samia gurgled, clawing at her hands.

The skin from Mina's hands were under her nails, she dug so deep.

Almost losing consciousness, Samia kicked her in the stomach so hard Mina doubled over. In pain, she held her lower abandon. Back in control, Samia grabbed her gun from out the waist of her jeans and pointed it at Mina's face. Mina stood frozen stiff. Samia was staring at her with a deranged look in her eyes. She was dressed from head to toe in all black. Samia was there to kill her.

"Samia, what are you doing?" Mina panted, confused.

"I'm doing what I should've done a long time ago. I'm gettin' rid of you so I can finally have everything I want." She cocked the hammer back.

Samia had taken it upon herself to off Mina. She'd failed at getting rid of Victor. She and Diego had created another plan to get rid of Victor and Mina at the same time, but Samia was tired of plotting and waiting. She wanted to get the dirty deed over with. The sooner the job was done, the closer they'd be to getting what they both wanted. Diego would be mad that she'd gone rogue but he'd forgive her once they had another drug empire in their grasp.

"First, I'll kill you… then Victor," she smiled devilishly.

"I thought you loved Victor?"

"I don't give a damn about Victor! He was just a part of my plan."

"What plan?" Mina tried to keep her talkin' so she could figure out her next move.

"To pay back my father for hurting me. Once I get Victor out the way, I'ma rule the world, bitch." She stepped closer.

"But your father is dead."

"Exactly; 'cause I killed him. Just like I'm going to kill you and Victor."

"Samia, wait! You don't want to do this." Mina stepped back.

Blood was dripping from her mouth.

"Shut the fuck up!" Samia jerked her hand. "You don't know what I want!"

"I know you want to be in Lelah's life. What about her? Think about what this will do to her. You don't wanna lose her again."

"I never wanted her! The only reason I had the little bitch is because Victor's family pressured me to! If I could've had it my way, she would've been sucked out after month two!"

This bitch is crazy, Mina ran into one of the salon chairs.

"Rest in peace, Mina. Now Victor really will know what it's like to have a dead wife." Samia went to fire the gun, but before she could pull the trigger, she was shot point blank in the back of the head.

A loud popping sound rang through the air, piercing Mina's ears. Blood splattered all over her face. Mina's body shook uncontrollably. She was in disbelief over what had just happened. Mina watched in horror as Samia gave her one last look and fell dead to the floor. Mina was so shaken up that she didn't know who the shooter was until Victor's security guard, Tony, appeared.

"You ok, Mrs. Gonzalez?" He asked stepping over Samia's limp body.

"No, I'm not ok. I'm not ok at all." Mina held her stomach and puked all over the floor.

Forgiveness:

The action or process of forgiving or being forgiven.

So now we're gonna heal.

#25

Tony helped Mina inside the house. Her lip was busted, and her ribs were severely bruised, but she was alive. Victor anxiously awaited her arrival. Tony had called him on the way there and told him everything. Victor was heated to say the least. He'd made plans to take care of Samia himself. He never wanted Mina to be involved in the drama. He wanted her to stay in the dark so he could shield her from any worry. Once again, hiding the truth from her nearly cost Mina her life. Victor realized that keeping secrets didn't do anyone any good. It only served his own purpose.

Mina limped through the door with her arm wrapped around Tony's neck. She held onto her ribs and winced in agony. Each step she took was like she was being kicked in the stomach all over again. She couldn't get the visual of Samia being murdered out of her head. Specks of her blood still remained on her face.

"Baby!" Victor sprinted over to help.

As soon as Mina saw him, she burst into tears. If it hadn't been for Tony, she would've been dead. She and Victor would've never gotten to see each other again. She wouldn't get to witness the wrinkle in his brow every time he smiled, or listen to him snore while he slept or treasure his forehead kisses. It all would've been taken away. All the fighting and silly games they'd play over the last few months had been a complete waste of time. It was petty and stupid. Sure, they had a lot to work through. The trust between the two of them had been broken, but with time, if they both put forth the effort, they could heal again.

"Victor!" Mina fell into his awaiting arms.

Victor held onto her for dear life. Dried tears stained her face. The smell of fresh blood permeated her clothes. It was so crystal clear to him. He needed Mina now and forever. He could never lose her again. All of the resentment and bullshit had melted away. He needed her right there by his side. It was time to show her all his cards and give her his heart.

Victor kissed her face, neck and lips. With every kiss, he thanked God that he hadn't taken her away. He wouldn't have been able to handle it. Without her, there was no him. Mina was his world. There was so much shit he had to say to her. He couldn't let another day go by where he didn't apologize for the sins he'd committed. From that day, moving forward, Victor vowed to pledge his undying love to her. He knew it would take time but he was determined to win back her trust.

"Is it handled?" He asked Tony while holding Mina in his arms.

Tony nodded his head. He'd called the cleaning crew. They went to the shop and disposed of Samia's body. When they were done, the salon didn't have any evidence that there had been a murder there. The death of Samia would remain between them.

"Anything else you need, Jefe?" Tony asked before leaving.

"Make sure the other guards are keeping an eye on the kids." Victor rocked Mina back and forth.

"Sure thing, boss." Tony closed the door behind him.

"Victor, what the fuck is going?" Mina asked.

Victor ran down the entire story; by the time he was done, Mina was experiencing sensory overload. She couldn't believe her ears. Bishop and Samia were plotting to take them out. Here Mina was thinking Victor was the enemy when Bishop was really the villain. She'd literally slept with the enemy.

"C'mon." Victor scooped Mina up in his arms. "Let's get you cleaned up."

Mina held on tight as he cradled her in his arms like a newborn baby. Victor already had a hot bath ready for her. No words were spoken between them as he took off her clothes - one item at a time. Mina was so troubled, she couldn't stop shaking. Victor hated seeing his sweet baby so distressed.

As he removed her clothes, he placed loving kisses all over her body. Victor made it his business to focus his full attention on the bruise on her right side. It was the size of a cantaloupe. Samia had gotten her good. Victor placed Mina's fragile body into the hot bubble bath. Mina let her body adjust to the temperature of the heat.

"I'll be right back." Victor assured. "I need to go get you a towel."

"Ok," Mina nodded as tears dripped from her bloodshot eyes.

She didn't want Victor to leave her alone. Samia was still torturing her through the grave. Flashes of the bullet going through Samia's skull kept replaying over and over in her mind. Mina didn't know how she'd ever be able to shake the horrific memory. Grabbing her head, she broke down and cried. Her warm, wet hands slid down her face. Mina slid her knees up to her chest and sat in the fetal position.

God said he wouldn't put more on you than you could handle, but Mina was past her limit. She was still mourning the death of her grandmother. Now she had to deal with almost being killed by her husband's psycho first wife. Victor tapped on the door to let her know he'd returned. Mina looked up at him. His strong presence soothed her. His beautiful face made a world of difference in her mood. Victor was gorgeous.

Victor held a stack of towels in his hands. Slowly, he walked over to the sink and placed them down. Mina never once took her eyes off of him. Victor got on his knees and ran his fingers through her wet hair. The short pieces of her hair curled from the water. Victor felt like shit. This was all his fault. If he'd never went searching for Samia, none of this would've happened.

Regretful tears fell from his eyes. He never thought they'd share a tender moment like this again. He thought he'd lost Mina for good. When she hit him with the divorce papers, he presumed that was the end for them. Victor didn't know how he was going to recover. He thought Mina was going to hate him forever. If she did, he couldn't blame her.

He'd let her down in the worst possible way. He'd sacrificed 10 years of marriage for what, a long-lost love he barely knew? Like most black men, he disregarded her feelings and cries for attention to satisfy his own selfish needs. He discarded his queen when she needed her king the most. As a man, he was supposed to move his queen forward, not hold her back and tear her down. His black queen was the definition of magic. Victor didn't want to be the man he'd been anymore.

He didn't want to be like the millions of other black men he knew that treated black women as if they were disposable. He didn't want to be like the other black men that tried to replace his black woman with something shinier and new. Black women were the backbone of the nation. They spun gold out of the hard life given to them. They were bulletproof. The only thing that could shoot them down was the black man. Mina had given him her blood, sweat and tears for years without asking for anything in return - besides his love and respect.

Victor was going to be better for her. With every tear he shed came redemption. They were going to start over. He'd cut her open, now it was time for him to put her back together again. No matter how long it took, he was going to love her fears and scars away.

Mina relished the touch of Victor's hand. Each touch felt like she was being baptized. It was time for the healing process to begin. But if they were going to try once more, it had to be glorious. They'd built sandcastles that washed away. Victor had broken her. He'd torn her down and shattered the illusion of the perfect life she thought they possessed. Now there they were, two broken souls trying to find redemption in the forgiveness of each other.

Through all the insanity, love still remained. She'd scratched out his name and his face but there was something about him that could not be erased. Maybe it was the way he gazed into her eyes as he peeled off his clothes and got in the tub with her. Victor knew only he could wash her fears away, so he did. He took the sponge and cleansed her body with ease.

With every stroke of his hand, Mina cried what seemed like a gallon of tears. Victor replaced the sponge with his lips. His mouth traveled up her leg and thigh to her breasts. Mina gasped. Her body still ached but his kisses made all of her pain disappear. Victor slid in between her legs. The water cascaded over the sides of the tub and splashed onto the floor. Mina enveloped his face with her wet hand.

"I'm sorry." Victor whispered as his lips devoured hers.

Mina gripped his muscular back as her tears mixed with his. Making love to Victor was the perfect remedy to what ached her soul. Victor rubbed his nose against hers as he slid deep inside her slit. Mina felt so good, he had to hold steady for a minute. It had been ages since he'd been inside his wife. When he was ready, he slowly wound his hips in a circular motion. Victor didn't want to rush a thing. He was going to take his time with her. The troubles of yesterday were gone. He didn't give a fuck that they'd broken up. Victor was gonna love Mina until the day he die.

Resurrection:

The action or fact of resurrecting or being resurrected.

You are terrifying… and strange… and beautiful.

#26

That same night, across town, HG Dance Club was the place to be. The vibe was all the way lit. HG aka The Horny Goat had a Miami appeal to it. Everything was white from the ceiling to the furniture. The club boast a sleek, modern design with a stage, VIP booths and several rentable booths. A metal hoop near the ceiling allowed for aerial acts.

Diego stood tall at his table with a bottle of Ace of Spades in hand, doing his thing. He and his mans had bought out the bar. Life was great. Everything was falling into place. In a matter of days, he and Samia would officially rule the world. No one in the drug game would be able to fuck with them. Together, they would have taken down and acquired two of the biggest and baddest drug cartels known to man.

Everyone thought Victor was smart and ruthless. So far, all Diego saw was a weak-ass man that didn't know how to satisfy his bitch. Diego thought he would be a formidable opponent, but Victor was nowhere on his level. He was still playing checkers while Diego played chess.

They were in two different weight classes. Diego felt like the man. His late father would've been proud.

Smoking a blunt, he caught the eye of a pretty girl dancing across the way. She'd been eye-fuckin' him since she stepped through the door. Babygirl was bad. She was black but had Spanish features. Her hair was cornrowed to the back. Heart-shaped, Bamboo earrings dangled from her ears. Mami was a pretty little thing. Chocolate skin, slim waist with a fat ass. Diego was a sucker for a chick with a fat ass. The way she twirled her hips and licked her lips just for him, had Diego thinking a lot of nasty things. Homegirl was giving him his very own private show right in the middle of the club.

Diego loved an uninhibited bitch. He was drunk off Henny and ready to fuck something. Li'l mama was sure to be his latest victim. Ready to get shit poppin', he gestured for her to come over. Shorty switched her ass hard as she approached him. Diego didn't waste any time. He cut straight to the point.

"I'm about to leave. You tryin' to come home with me or what?" He asked with an intense look of desire in his eyes.

"Damn, you bold. Hi. How you doing?" The girl stuck out her hand.

"What's good wit' you?" He took her hand and pulled her close. His hard dick rested on her stomach. "What's your name?"

"Renee," she smiled, taking in his army fatigue Bathing Ape jacket, Calvin Klein boxer/briefs and Dsquared jeans. "What's yours?"

"Bishop," Diego lied.

"I see you, Bishop" Renee sucked her teeth, pleased with what she saw.

His jacket was wide open. Bishop had no shirt on underneath. His chest full of tattoos had her turned on to the fullest. Plus, the light was hittin' his Rolex right.

"But for real. What you about to get into? 'Cause I'm about to dip."

"Me and my girls," she pointed across her shoulder. "Was just about to hit up Illusions for some chicken."

"Won't you come back to the crib wit' me?" Diego held her by the waist. "We ain't gotta do nothin'. We could just chill. Smoke a L or something." He lied, again.

He and Renee were most definitely fuckin'.

Renee thought about it for a second. Homeboy was fine as fuck and he was iced out. Fucking a nigga like him would be just like winning the jackpot. She would at least get an orgasm, some food and a few dollars out the deal.

"A'ight. Let me tell my girls I'm leaving."

Once they left the club, Diego stopped by a gas station to get a box of condoms. Raw was never the way he got down. Never the one to let a bitch know where he laid his head, he copped a room at the Renaissance Hotel by the airport. The hotel was nice enough to let her know he wasn't no slouch in the financial department. A bird bitch like Renee, that fucked a nigga within a minute of meeting him, would be impressed. Diego and Renee hit the elevator, blunted. He hadn't eaten all day, so Henny was the only thing in his system.

Inside the hotel room, he stripped down to his boxer/briefs. Diego placed his chains, Rolex and phone on the night table by the bed. Renee followed suit and came out of her clothes. Babygirl had a body like a stripper. Her 34 DD breasts sat nice and firm, but her apple bottom ass was what drew him in the most. Her ass was heavy. The visual of gripping her waist and hitting it from behind as her ass jiggled was amazing. Ripples of flesh danced before his eyes. He was mesmerized.

Diego fucked Renee in every position imaginable. When they were done, they both lay spent, smoking a blunt. He learned that she never fucked with sour weed but loved purple. She fucked a couple niggas but didn't believe in love. Renee was from the Westside, went to hair school and had two kids by a nigga that used to like to beat on her.

Diego wasn't really into the semantics but he let her talk. He figured they'd order some room service and fuck twice. But halfway through the conversation, he zoned out. It was going on 3:00am. The Hennessey mixed with weed had him buggin'. Before Diego knew it, he was passed out. An hour later, there was a knock on the door.

"Room service!"

Diego didn't remember ordering anything to eat. He figured Renee did. When he turned over to tell her to get the door, he realized she was gone. Diego groggily sat up, confused. Renee was M.I.A and all her shit was gone. There was no trace of her clothes, purse or shoes anywhere. Homegirl had dipped.

He didn't really give a fuck that she'd left. It saved him the trouble of having to do the dirty work of tossing her a few dollars for cab fare so she could get the fuck outta there. Diego was chill until he peeped that his shit was gone too. His heart began to race. All of his chains, Rolex, iPhone - all gone. Diego checked his jeans. The bitch had even taken his gun, his wallet with his bank cards and the 10 grand that was inside his pocket.

Diego put his clothes on. He was ready to murder Renee. That sneaky bitch had a bullet to the head with her name on it. Shit like this didn't happen to men like him. He hadn't even drunk that much. How in the fuck did he get robbed? Pissed, Diego raced to the door to see if the hotel employee had seen her. As soon as he opened it, he was stopped dead in his tracks. To his surprise and utter dismay, Victor stood before him. He didn't need a whole crew of niggas to support him. When Victor had to put in work, he did his dirt all by his lonely.

"Going somewhere?" He asked coldly.

After making love to his wife, he dipped out once Mina had fallen asleep. There wouldn't be another day that passed by that Diego Vasquez got to live on earth. He'd caused enough turmoil and strife to his life. Plus, he'd fucked his wife. Diego had to go. Victor was getting rid of his ass that night. Muthafuckas could come for him all they wanted, but when they involved his wife, all bets were off.

Diego's skin went pale. All the blood drained from his face. Victor was finally on to him. His number was up. Victor didn't say another word. His 9mm pistol with a silencer would do all the talking. With not a hint of remorse or trepidation, Victor pulled the trigger and shot Diego three times in the head. He watched, expressionless, as his body collapsed to the floor. Seeing that he was dead, Victor pocketed his gun and made his way out the building via the hotel fire exit. Tony was outside awaiting his return. Victor hopped in the passenger seat of his all-black SUV and Tony sped off.

"Everything good, Jefe?" Julissa asked from the backseat, as she took the braids she'd been wearing that night out of her head.

"Never been better, Renee."

Hope:

A feeling of expectation and desire for a
certain thing to happen.

"I made you cry when I walked away."

-Beyoncé, "Sandcastles"

#27

The next morning when Mina awake, her body felt as if it had been hit by a Mack truck. Victor had given her a pill for the pain that knocked her out. Unfortunately for her, the pill had worn off. Mina winced as soon as she turned over. She was surprised when she learned that she was in bed alone. Mina looked around for Victor but found a stack of envelopes wrapped in a white satin ribbon on his pillow instead.

Confused as to what the envelopes could be, she eased up into the sitting position and placed them on her lap. The letters were addressed to her and the sender was Victor. He'd written her over ten letters that he'd never mailed. Mina untied the ribbon and opened the letter on top. Inside she read a handwritten letter from Victor that said:

Mina,

You asked me to write you a love letter so here I go. I'm not the best at expressing my feelings but, baby, before I met you all my days were spent in silent contemplation of what was lacking in my life and why real love seemed to evade me. The second you told me you loved me, all my doubts and reservations went away. I knew for a fact that I found what I had been lookin' for all along. Baby, your love made me realize the best thing life had to offer, and with that knowledge, I knew that my life was complete. I may not express it each day but I just want to tell you that you are special to me.

Mina tried her best not to cry as she read the next letter.

Baby, I know I'm a difficult man to handle, and you've had a tough time dealin' wit' me during our marriage. I may come across moody at times, but believe me, my love for you will stay pure till the end of time. With you, I'm getting to know a special part of me.

By the time Mina got to the third letter, she was bawling. Tears dripped from her eyes onto the paper.

Mina,

I've been having sleepless nights. I think about you day and night. I can't get you out of my mind. It's like you have taken over my mind and have formed your kingdom there. Nothing else gives me peace like your face. Your voice, your charm and your advice is all that I need to go on with life. I can't be away from you any longer. Life without you is like food without salt. I need you to be there for me and guide me. I want to be the reason you smile and the reason you're happy to wake up in the morning. I promise to always take care of you and your heart. Please say that you'll be mine forever. I'll do whatever it takes to make things right with you.

Victor

Mina's heart fluttered inside of her chest. In the 10 years she and Victor had been together, he'd never done anything sweeter. He'd given her diamonds, cars, and clothes and had taken her on trips around the world, but these simple love letters were by far the best gift she could've ever received.

"I see you found the letters." Victor stood in the doorway.

He'd been watching her for a minute.

"Victor," Mina choked up.

"Don't cry." He came over to her side of the bed and got down on his knees.

Victor took her hand in his and held on for dear life.

"Baby, I'm sorry. I never meant to hurt you. I swear to God on everything I love I'll never do it again."

Mina wiped her eyes. Her head said don't believe him but her heart wasn't willing to let go of her man. She loved Victor with all of her heart. Trust wouldn't come overnight. He'd have to earn it again with time. The point was that Mina was willing to give him the opportunity to.

"I love you too."

Time heals all wounds. Which is what Mina had been told all of her life. The older she got, the more she realized how true the statement was. The bruises she received from her fight with Samia vanished after a few weeks. When the kids saw her in such a battered and bruised state, they went out of their minds. She and Victor told them she'd been in a severe car accident. The kids were shaken up but happy their mother was alive. They did everything in their power to make sure she was comfortable.

When Lelah didn't hear from Samia after a while, she began to wonder what had happened to her. Mina and

Victor sat her down and broke the news to her that Samia had faked her death the first time and now had disappeared again. Lelah kind of figured her parents were lying to her. It wasn't a coincidence that Mina came home looking like the Walking Dead and her biological mother disappeared around the same time.

Lelah was a big girl. She figured something tragic had happened but didn't press the subject for answers. Her parents were trying to protect her for a reason. She had to respect that. It was nice to get to know her mother, but when it all boiled down, Samia was never really her family. If she had to choose between her and Mina, Mina would win every time. She was her mom and anybody that put her mother in harm's way was dead to her.

Mina's life was finally getting back on track. With everything that had happened, she found herself missing Nana Marie like crazy. She was normally the one she ran to when times got rough. Mina now had to find solace during troubled times within herself. With each breath she took, she pulled herself back together again. The journey of reconciliation with her husband wasn't an easy one.

She couldn't wipe away months of anger and pain that resided behind her hazel eyes with a mere snap of the finger. Mina would need time to prove that she could trust Victor again. It wouldn't be easy, but she was willing to give it a fighting chance. After 10 years of being together, he deserved a second chance. Most women would've been like hell no and threw in the towel, but marriage was never an easy thing. It was nasty at times, confusing, stressful and tiring. Disagreements led to resentment. Resentment then transformed to hate.

Marriage was all about compromise. It was about setting your pride aside and loving someone despite their flaws. Victor was her best friend, the father of her children, her protector. He'd seen the deepest, darkest parts of her soul and loved her anyway. When he walked back into her life, Mina realized why she could never make it work with anyone else. She was placed on earth to love him. He was the man that brought salvation back into her soul. Before him, Mina always had a smart and practical way at looking at love. With him, nothing made sense.

There was no controlling her emotions. Behind the veil of a flawless smile and rock-hard abs was a man that loved her truly and deeply. He would lay down his life for her. Victor wasn't perfect by any means necessary, but he was perfect for her. He was the only man that could turn her insides to mush and make her stomach flutter. He made her feel safe and comfortable in her own skin. So, they were going to do what they should've done from the beginning and tear down the barrier that kept them apart. Together, they were going to stop this love drought.

Redemption:

The action of saving or being saved from
sin, error, or evil.

My torturer became my remedy.

#28

Eight months later, Victor took Mina by the hand and led her out onto the dance floor. All of the couples at Mo and Boss' wedding were dancing to Beyoncé's *All Night*. The song always put a smile on Mina's face. Victor had his baby back and he was never letting her go. She was an addiction he couldn't shake. Mina was his only virtue. She was priceless. The possibilities between them were endless. Together, they'd found the truth behind his lies. They still had their days were they went for each other's throats, but their love for each other overshadowed any drama they had.

Mina looked over at her friend. Mo was the happiest she'd ever been. Months earlier, she'd had her fourth child, which was a boy they named Zaire, after his father. Mo's body was already back into tip-top shape. The floral-embroidered, Zac Posen, wedding gown and veil she wore was breathtaking. Mo was by far the prettiest bride she'd ever seen, outside of herself.

The months of planning her wedding had paid off. Over 200 people were there. Everyone was in awe of the reception venue. It was like they were in a winter wonderland. Billows of white flowers hovered over the tables like clouds. Lace table linen and rustic-inspired center pieces decorated each table.

Victor twirled his wife around in a circle. Her pregnant belly looked so cute inside her black bridesmaid dress. Mina was almost due to have their baby girl. God had a funny way of making things happen during his own timing. When they'd wanted a baby, she couldn't get pregnant.

When they weren't even trying, she was able to conceive. The baby was a blessing to their life. Mina couldn't wait to hold their baby girl in her arms. She and Victor had decided to name her Savannah Marie Gonzalez in honor of Nana Marie. Mina was sure that she was her baby's guardian angel. Victor and Mina swayed to the music.

"How I've missed you, my love." She nuzzled her face against his.

Mina never wanted to let him go. They'd survived hell. Everything they did now made sense. For him, she shared a cup of love that overflowed. There was no low or high of her heart that he hadn't seen. Mina was in it for eternity. She was served lemons but she'd made lemonade. She'd figured out the antidote. Nothing real could be threatened. There are no small decisions in life. Every decision that you make effects who you are and every action that you take or don't take has consequences and it effects the people around you.

Victor had shattered her illusion of him. He became her torturer and then her torturer became her remedy. He'd made the woman in doubt disappear. Love was no longer an illusion. She'd discovered the real person behind the magic veil. Love was an endless book. You never know what is going to happen next. There is no table of context, glossary or how to manual. Love was a mystery. You just have to turn one page at a time and hold on for the ride.

The End

057833213

CPSIA information can be obtained
at www.ICGtesting.com
Printed in the USA
LVOW13s1738250817

546379LV00005B/689/P